PRAISE FOR *BACK IN BROOKFORD*

"*Back in Brookford* isn't just a stellar collection of short stories, it's a dark and poignantly funny portrait of a small town and its inhabitants, reminiscent of *Winesburg, Ohio* and *American Graffiti*. David Lott is a wise and compassionate observer of his characters and the community that formed them."

—TOM PERROTTA

New York Times bestselling author of *Mrs. Fletcher*
and *The Leftovers*

"David Lott's *Back in Brookford* is something of a miracle. In a series of overlapping tales, Lott introduces us to a cast of characters trying to make their way in a fictional town that is at once unforgettable and indistinguishable from thousands of similar communities across the country. The people in these tales are grappling with their sexuality, with failing marriages, with hunger and bullying and boredom. But this is also a work of daring, as Lott takes us from the 1960s to the present to the future. In prose that is vigorous and direct, and with an eye for the perfect detail, Lott has created a book that will bring to mind Sherwood Anderson's *Winesburg, Ohio*, but that speaks uniquely to our fractured times. With *Back in Brookford*, Lott joins the ranks of Tom Perrotta, Brando Skyhorse, Gloria Naylor, Lauren Groff, and so many other great writers who have given us vivid portraits of uniquely American spaces and the way they shape us."

—WILL SCHWALBE

New York Times bestselling author of *The End of Your Life Book Club* and *Books for Living*

BACK
IN
BROOKFORD

BACK
IN
BROOKFORD

Stories

....

DAVID LOTT

NICHOLS STREET PRESS

A NICHOLS STREET PRESS PUBLICATION

Text design and layout by Michelle McMillian

"Great to Meet You!" was originally published, in slightly different form, in *MonkeyBicycle*. "Glut Hut" and "Honeysuckle" were originally published, in slightly different form, in *96th of October*.

ISBN 978-0-578-35488-0 (trade paperback original)
ISBN 978-0-578-35489-7 (ebook)

First Edition

For Jenny

CONTENTS

Facts and Figures

FROM CASSIE MAYBAUGH'S "ME-TIME" BLOG

2015

And lastly, I've talked (and *talked*) to a lot of y'all, and everyone seems to agree that an "All Alumni" reunion is the way to go next summer. So any and *all* graduates of Brookford High are invited. We're shooting for mid July. More details to come.

In the meantime, I've copied and pasted below some facts and figures about Brookford I found on megapedia.com. A lot of it is pretty dry, so I've dropped in some comments of my own. Hope these will give people a better idea of the "real" Brookford *and* will also bring back some memories and get everybody excited about the reunion.

CITY OF BROOKFORD

- Incorporated: 1834
- Population: 19,237

  Love the size of our "small town," but I always thought

our population was 20,000 on the nose. Can't we convince 763 people to move down the road from Turnersburg? :)

- Founded: 1795, by Gen. Jonas Z. Warren
- Motto: "Brookford: A Great Place to Visit, a Wonderful Place to Live"

  <u>Wonderful</u> *with a capital W. Lakes and mountains and rivers—God's country, y'all. And so much better than dealing with smoggy city traffic and drive-by's and who knows what all else going on in the "progressive" big cities.*

Geography:

- Elevation: 1601 feet (part of the state's Central Valley region)

  Rocky Mountain HIGH! (I know it's not quite that high . . . but still <u>high</u> enough!)

- Land area: 23.4 square miles

  That's a lot of acres. I read on megapedia that the original Scotch-Irish settlers measured the land in hectares. 23 square miles has got to be a lot of hectares too.

Notable Geographical Features:

- Lake Pamunkey, recreational lake approximately eight miles north of Brookford

  Our kids used to <u>live</u> at the lake in the summer when they were growing up. My youngest always joked about having a monkey in his pamunkey! Never knew what that meant—not sure I wanted to know—but we loved the fun times we had there.

- Mount Warren: small mountain/monadnock immediately east of Brookford; elevation: 2,388 feet

  Not to mention the fun times we had partying at the top of ol' Mount Warren in high school. Someone mentioned "keggers" the other day, but I don't think we ever really called them that. We just said, "Party at the tip-top." Everyone knew where to go.

  BTW, they're planning to renovate the entire scenic view area soon.

- Parallel mountain ranges approximately fifteen miles east and twenty miles west of Brookford, respectively.

  Like I said, lakes and mountains and rivers.

Climate:

- The climate in the area is characterized by hot, humid summers and generally mild to cool winters.

  This made me laugh: "mild to cool winters"—like when we got 20 feet of snow two years ago? Did someone say global WARMING? (I know it's called "climate change" now—and I do believe the scientists are probably right about all that. Still, when you're shoulder-deep in snow for three months—in the South!—it's hard to imagine that the Earth is getting hotter.)

Nearest Town/City:

- Turnersburg: Brookford's "Big Sister City"; population: 31,802

  Evil stepsister city, lol. But seriously, I do like Turners-

burg, right next to the mountains—even if it is the Land of the Almighty Mall. :) Wait, what am I talking about? I <u>love</u> the Almighty Mall.

Most Common Occupations:

- **Management (14%)**
- **Sales and related (13%)**
- **Construction and extraction (9%)**

  And farming. Thank the Good Lord for all the farm-land—and farmers—around Brookford.

Colleges/Universities:

- **Valley Community College**

  VCC! Woop, woop!

- **Brookford-Turnersburg International School of Makeup, Cosmetology, and Barbering**

  BTISMCB! Woop, woop!

Public and Private High School(s):

- **Brookford High School (public), "Home of the Bucks"**

  Yes! Or as we used to say (sorry, y'all): "Home of the F#%*ing Bucks"! ("'cause we will f#%* the other team up")

- **Elliott Gap High School (public; county)**
- **Harrison Cutler Preparatory Academy (private; co-ed)**

Most Common Outdoor Leisure Activities:

- Camping: year-round

  Not me. I went on a "February Frostbite" campout with the Girl Scouts back in 6th or 7th grade. Never again. I absolutely love the outdoors—bring me along on a picnic or a mountain hike any day of the year—but I want to sleep in my own comfy bed at night, thank you very much.

- Golfing: King Hill Park (par 3); Sunnyside Golf and Country Club
- Hiking: Mount Warren—designated 1, 2, and 5 mile trails
- Skiing: limited number of small lodges east of Turnersburg

  I hate to say it, but there's better skiing in my backyard, lol.

- Swimming (summer): King Hill Park; Lake Pamunkey—swimming lessons; swim league

Notable Locations:

- Brookford Public Library

  They keep BOOKS here. Remember those?

- Commerce Square business park
- Downtown "City Centre"

  Seriously? Megapedia lists the glorified bus stop on Lee-Jackson Avenue as a Notable Location? We need better Notable Locations! I guess, though, the City Centre does have Gloria's Ice Cream Shoppe and Ray's Stationery and the Arts Café. But still . . .

- King Hill Park: multi-use recreational park with picnic/ cookout facilities; public swimming pool; bicycle rentals
- Sunnyside Golf and Country Club

  Mostly a bunch of old guys smacking their balls around. Ha! My husband, Zack Bloomgarden ("Dr. B"), is one of them . . . Maybe we need a Cloudy Side Golf and Country Club for the rest of us.

Notable Events/Festivals:
- "The Arts Café Presents": monthly film presentation and discussion
- Brookford summer farmers market

  The absolute best/healthiest/freshest food <u>anywhere</u>: produce, cheese, breads, pies. Again, love the farmers.

- "Downtown DANCE!": bi-annual music festival

  I overheard someone recently refer to this as the Battle of the Bands, but I think it's the Battle of the DJs these days, sigh . . .

- Téatro: Brookford Amateur Theatre Company

  Summer performances under the stars are a must-see— everything from Shakespeare to Broadway. "They say the neon lights are bright . . ."

Okay, kids, that's it for now. I'm really getting psyched for next summer! Hope you are too.

  C U sooooon . . .

BACK
IN
BROOKFORD

Redhead

After the little girl spent the day at her friend Samantha Drinkwater's house—and Samantha's mother let the two of them run a lemonade stand in the front yard—the little girl's own mother promised (promised!) that soon she could set one up at home too.

The little girl, named Ruth after her great-grandma, waited. She played with her dolls in the cool damp of the basement when her mother needed her to be quiet for an hour or two. She rode along with her mother on all her errands. To the drugstore, the A&P, sometimes to her mother's friend Shirley's place so that her mother and Shirl could sit on the back porch and visit, sipping sweet tea and smoking cigarettes while Ruth watched the television inside. Her mother and Shirl whispered a lot too. Occasionally her mother cried.

Ruth didn't like upsetting her mother, but sometimes she

couldn't stand the waiting and had to ask about the lemonade stand. Her mother's face would turn ugly. "I said *soon*. Keep bothering me about it and maybe we won't have a lemonade stand at all," she'd say.

But then, at the very end of the summer, on the day before Ruth was to start first grade, her mother called her into the kitchen. "I don't know what I was thinking agreeing to this foolishness," she said. "But if your heart's set on it, I guess it'll have to be today."

Samantha's mother had squeezed a big lump of frozen lemonade from a can, and Ruth asked if they could do the same. She held her breath, afraid her mother might make her ugly face. But her mother just ran her fingers through Ruth's hair like she sometimes did and said, "No, little girl, I thought we'd make ours from scratch, all right?"

From a cabinet above the stove, Ruth's mother brought down her see-through ice-tea pitcher. She emptied an entire tray of ice into it, filled it with water, and poured in what was left of a sack of sugar. From the icebox, she took a tall green bottle. "Real juice," she said, before measuring out some in a cup and pouring that into the pitcher too.

After stirring the mixture with a long wooden spoon, she let Ruth take a sip. Ruth decided right then that lemonade from scratch was not her favorite. Slightly sweet, it mostly made her lips and tongue tingle. Not wanting to disappoint her mother, though, she kept quiet. Besides, the lemonade wasn't for her anyway; it was for the people who'd be stopping by her stand. If lemonade from scratch was what everyone liked, she was happy to be giving them what they wanted.

On the front stoop, Ruth's mother turned a cardboard box upside down and set the pitcher of lemonade on top of it, along with a stack of paper cups. She helped Ruth write on the side of the box with a purple crayon, in big letters: "Lemonade—5 cents." Ruth was pleased to see, when she went out to the curb and looked back, that the letters showed up even that far away.

The sun beat down on Ruth and her mother as they sat on the top step next to the box, Ruth in her sleeveless blue party dress, her mother wearing a yellow blouse and bright checkered shorts. Ruth heard the rush of traffic a few blocks away on Lee-Jackson Avenue, but no cars turned onto their street. No one was strolling along the sidewalk either. After a while, her mother stood up, saying in her no-nonsense voice that it was time to go in. "It's just too hot, little girl. Nobody wants to be outside on a miserable day like this."

Ruth knew better than to contradict her mother but couldn't help herself. She asked if she couldn't please sit there for a little while longer. Someone was certain to pass by, and when they did she wanted to have a cold drink ready for them. She and Samantha had sold lemonade to several people, including an elderly lady who'd said how wonderful it was that young children were there, at the ready, waiting to provide relief to the "parched and weary." Ruth liked the way the lady smiled and spoke to her and Samantha.

"A few more minutes and that's it," her mother said.

"I'm going to go lay down. You are not to leave this stoop, you understand me?"

Ruth nodded.

Once the screen door had slapped shut behind her mother, Ruth leaned forward as far as she could, squinting up and down the street. She called "Lemonade" in a soft voice and then, louder, "Lemonade!" An airplane whined somewhere above her in the empty white sky, and she tried to spot it. But the sky was so bright that before long she had to look away, squeezing her eyes shut.

When she opened them, a man was standing in front of her. Tall, with thick arms and a big belly. A wedge of pale skin showed between his T-shirt and belt. Ruth was surprised: She hadn't seen a car drive up, and nobody had been walking toward her just seconds earlier.

"Hey there," the man said in a low voice, glancing between Ruth and the house. "I think I know your name, so don't tell me." The clothes he wore looked old. Ruth noticed that the knees of his trousers were ripped and dirty.

"Betty, right?" he said, with a huge grin, like he was proud of himself. He smelled smoky, but at the same time almost sweet, like the short, bald man at the A&P who put out the tomatoes and peaches and always said hello to Ruth and her mother. She liked how nice that man was. This man seemed nice too.

"No, it's Ruth," she said.

"Aw, now, I said don't tell me. 'Ruth' was gonna be my second guess." He kept grinning for a couple of seconds but then got a serious look on his face.

Ruth hadn't meant to ruin the game. She wondered if the man was mad. "I'm sorry," she whispered. When he didn't say anything back—maybe he hadn't heard her—she spoke up and asked if he'd like to try some lemonade.

This time he did hear her, and he looked down at the overturned box and Ruth's sign. "I tell you what," he said, "I'll take a cup and you can keep the change." He dug in his pocket and pulled out a dime.

Ruth poured his lemonade without spilling a drop, like she'd learned to do at Samantha's. The man took a sip before gulping the rest. "Mm-hmm," he said. "I bet your momma helped you make that." He squatted so that his face was directly in front of Ruth's. "Anyone ever tell you that you look just like her?"

Ruth shook her head. She wasn't sure whether the man was still playing a guessing game. She suddenly didn't feel like answering.

"Well, you do. You look *just* like her." The man's face got funny. His eyes got red and watery. Ruth's stomach started hurting, the same as when her mother cried on Shirl's porch. She hated that feeling. It made tears fill her eyes too.

The man held up a finger like he was trying to shush her. "Don't cry, I'm not gonna hurt you." Without saying anything more, he reached out and put his big hands on Ruth's shoulders. She knew he wasn't supposed to do this, but his hands actually felt fine, cool on her skin as he rested them there.

After several moments, he gave her shoulders a squeeze and stood up again. "It was a real pleasure meeting you,

Ruth, but I think I best be going." He eyed the house once more. "I'll see you again, though, all right?" He took a couple of steps backward, then turned and crossed the street. Halfway down the block, he glanced over his shoulder at her before hopping a fence and disappearing into the pine woods on the other side of it.

Ruth sat outside another minute, watching the woods, wondering if the man might come back. She wasn't crying anymore but knew she should tell her mother what had happened.

Standing at the edge of her mother's bed, Ruth said a man had come by and bought lemonade. Her mother barely moved beneath the sheets. When Ruth told her what the man had said, though, her mother sat straight up. "He said what?"

"He got real close to me and said I looked just like you." Ruth didn't want to tell her mother he'd touched her. Nobody was allowed to do that, and she'd be angry.

Her mother got out of bed. "Oh my God. What else did he say?" She raised the window shade and peered outside.

"Nothing," Ruth said.

Her mother turned from the window, eyes wide, scaring Ruth for a moment. But Ruth thought of something she knew would make her mother feel better. "He said I looked like you, but he's wrong. My hair isn't black like yours is." She paused, picturing the man again. "I'm a redhead, Momma. Like him."

Glut Hut

RUTH EASTMAN MAKES A PROMISE

1998

Christopher Eastman leans across the front passenger seat, framing himself in the window as he waves goodbye. Daniel, giddy in his straitjacket booster seat, waves too, wiggling all of his pudgy little fingers. Then they're off. Christopher's gold Lexus LS, the car he bought last year after his chain of beer-themed restaurants did so well, sails down the oil-black driveway, the sound of the engine soon lost in the wind that gusts through the tall hemlocks beside the house.

His wife, Ruth, continues to wave back at them, certain that Christopher is watching her in his rearview, that Daniel is straining to look over his shoulder for a final glimpse of Mommy. She continues to wave even after the Lexus has hopped the hump at the base of the long drive, between the squat marble columns, on the way to Christopher's father's place for a boys-only weekend of stock-pond fishing and visiting Krauss's apple orchard. Only after it's vanished around the bend in the road does she drop her arm, turn, and step along the walk to the front door, already missing her guys, wondering whether she should have pressed harder to tag along on the trip. What if Daniel gets homesick, or calls out at three in the morning needing her to rescue him from a nightmare?

On the polished-stone landing in front of the house, Ruth stops. Her worrying has caused the knot of congestion in her chest—all that remains of the cold she came down with two weeks ago—to feel suddenly tight. She clears her throat for several moments before taking her long red hair in one hand, leaning over the side railing, and spitting into the tentacles of the ornamental razor grass, which sway under the front windows like seaweed anchored to the bottom of the ocean.

And she feels better. Freer. She can't help glancing behind her, though, with a vague sense she's being watched, that someone might have seen her disgusting hawking and spitting. But the house sits dead center on a large square tract of wooded land miles outside of town. Eleven acres, for heaven's sake. Ruth could dance naked on one of the high widow's-walk balconies, and not even her closest neighbors a quarter mile down the hill would see her.

This thought gives her an unexpected thrill, and a jolt of courage, and she opens the front door and goes inside to change.

Fifteen minutes later, she's in her own car, her cute emerald Porsche 911 Carrera, speeding along Pheasant Hunt Drive and Tally Ho Lane and Puddle Duck Hiway. The backcountry roads, as she and Christopher like to call them.

The tires hum over the asphalt, causing her bottom and the backs of her thighs to jiggle pleasantly. She enjoys the sensation but puts it out of her mind, wanting to delay gratification of any sort until she gets where she's going.

She's dressed down, in blue jeans, cowboy boots, and an old mustard-colored barn coat of Christopher's. A brown-plaid scarf covers her head. Large, black-rimmed shades hide most of her face. She doubts she'll run into anyone but doesn't want to risk being recognized. She tells herself, in fact, that the Porsche works as part of her disguise: Her mommy friends and the women she knows at church are more used to seeing her in her Land Cruiser, out shopping or idling in the parking lot of Daniel's pre-school.

She drives fast, the woods and hills of that part of the county soon behind her. Whizzing by now, too close to the road, are shabby ranch houses on one side, clusters of run-down row houses on the other. Pickup trucks sit in the short gravel drives; plastic jumbo play sets take up the tiny front yards. Ruth hates remembering her childhood in a neighborhood similar to this and doesn't ease off the accelerator until she's reached the south side of Brookford, a particularly commercial stretch of Lee-Jackson Avenue, where it's all convenience marts and strip malls and auto-repair shops.

Just beyond the first traffic light, she turns into the parking lot of Frannie's 4-Star Diner, which has been there since she was a little girl. She parks in the rear, backing into a slot a couple of spaces over from the restaurant's giant blue dumpster.

The new glut hut is behind the restaurant, on the other side of a brown-grass median, where the old Record Zone used to be. Off the main drag, thank goodness. Ruth noticed ads for it in a local arts paper and cruised by several times when she was out running errands. She sees its flat roof above the dumpster.

Her stomach is all nerves, and her chest starts to tighten again. She sits for a minute lightly rubbing her knuckles along the steering wheel. She glances at her manicured fingertips, noting with shame the stubby nail of her right thumb, which she's been gnawing. And her rings! She'd meant to leave them at home. Her pear-shaped diamond, her sapphires, her aquamarine. With a frustrated sigh, she swivels them off and hides them in the empty ashtray. Then, after checking her mirrors to make sure no one is close by, she gets out, locks the car, and walks across the median.

The windows of the two-story building are painted over from the inside, a darker shade of storm-cloud gray than the worn siding. Like the other glut huts Ruth's visited— the few in Turnersburg over the years and the one out by the interstate before Daniel was born—the word *Glut* is stenciled in red script lettering at the base of one of the windows, the only giveaway of what the building is used for.

Just as she catches her reflection in the same window— proud, for a brief moment, that despite her occasional binges, she has managed to keep herself relatively fit and trim, desirable even—an exhaust fan above the front door blows an oily-smelling wind into her face. Suddenly ashamed, she lowers her eyes, not wanting to look at herself a second longer. What in God's name is she doing here after all? She can't imagine what Christopher would think. For once, why not simply turn around and walk away?

At that moment, the door opens. A wiry young man with a triangle of blue fuzz on his chin, and wearing a pleated paper chef's hat, is saying hello, come in, come in. Ruth is surprised at how friendly and welcoming he seems, and she manages to whisper a thank-you. She removes her sunglasses and follows him inside.

The first-floor eatery is a surprise too, cleaner than others she's been to. And more colorful and inviting, like a comfortable neighborhood tavern. A collection of lava lamps crowds one end of a long Formica counter. Overhead, rows of track lighting shine spots of soft color around the room. It strikes Ruth that this, ironically enough, is the very type of ambience that Christopher has been aiming for with his restaurants. She makes a mental note to mention this to him, before catching herself, knowing that she can never say anything about this place to her husband. Again she fights off the urge to leave. After taking a deep breath, she pushes thoughts of home from her mind and instead tries her best to focus on her surroundings.

She notices the smell of fried chicken even before she sees it listed, along with pizza and donuts, on a small chalk-board next to the counter. At least the offerings—always fried chicken, pizza, and donuts—are as expected. This is a comfort to Ruth, and she allows herself to relax a bit as the young man, behind the counter now in a white apron, asks what he can get for her. She orders her usual, three cheese slices and two Boston creams. When she asks if there's soup, the man's smile widens. Of course, he tells her, and starts to rattle off items from their specialty menu: gourmet stews, overstuffed sandwiches, dipping sauces—also, a variety of pies, cakes, puddings . . . She interrupts, saying a large serving of plain tomato will be fine.

He bows slightly and disappears through a swinging door into the kitchen, returning minutes later with Ruth's food on an orange-plastic tray, asking if her order is for the glut.

Ruth nods. What else would the food be for? She can't imagine anyone, any regular—normal—person, stopping by just to sample the menu.

The young man rings up her total on the cash register, saying very good, ma'am, and telling her that she has thirty minutes upstairs, unless she would like to add more time. Ruth says no, and after paying him takes her change, receipt, and tray.

The smell of ammonia stings her nose as she climbs the staircase. At the top, an obese, sixtyish woman in a yellowing housedress sits behind a wooden desk that's been painted pink. In front of her are a half-empty two-liter bottle of Mountain Dew and a paper plate strewn with chicken bones. At first, Ruth thinks a wad of grape bubble gum is somehow stuck to the woman's mouth, but then she sees that it's the woman's lips, pursed and swollen purple. Avoiding the woman's eyes, Ruth balances one edge of her tray on the front of the desk, slides her receipt across it, and asks which booth. The woman mumbles for her to take her pick.

Ruth heads toward the far end of the large, dimly lit room, where a line of private stalls is built into the wall, resembling a row of porta-potties.

On the way, she passes bin after bin of magazines and videotapes. Framed color photos hang on the walls, over-sized close-ups of watermelons, cantaloupes, and mangos, split open and dripping juice; a pitcher of fudge sauce being poured over a chocolate triple-layer cake; barbecued slabs of meat sputtering on a grill.

Generic soft rock plays through speakers in the ceiling, but no sounds are coming from any of the stalls. Figuring she's the only person there, Ruth pokes her head into a few before deciding on one at the end of the row that looks clean and has a tall wastebasket with a fresh plastic liner.

After setting her tray on a shelf that juts out from the left wall, she closes the stall door behind her and slides the latch that locks it. A lower shelf serves as a narrow seat in the dark, cramped space, but Ruth prefers to stand. She picks up her Styrofoam container of soup and blows across the surface. The television screen on the wall opposite the door remains black for a moment, then flickers to life.

The first images are from the movie *Tommy*: Ann-Margret writhes on the floor as a thousand gallons of baked beans and chocolate syrup spew all over her. Ruth has watched this scene before, and others from mainstream films—*Nine and a Half Weeks, Like Water for Chocolate,* even *Willy Wonka*—but they've never held much interest for her. She pushes the glowing green channel button on the wall beside the screen.

Next, a group of Japanese teenagers in kamikaze outfits gorge themselves on sushi, noodles, and rice. Ruth's seen more than enough eating contests, live events with drunk frat boys chugging marinara sauce and white gravy; home-made videos of suburban block parties where couples vie against their neighbors, speed-eating mayonnaise and pea-nut butter out of the jar. At the end of each contest, a big communal tub is wheeled in for anyone who needs to purge. Ruth flips the channel before the sushi-eaters get that far, amazed that anyone could enjoy witnessing such a thing.

Pilgrims-gone-wild is a popular theme, and on the screen now a dozen men and women gather around a picnic table at an urban park. Most wear black Pilgrim robes and hats; three of the men sport feathered headdresses and red loin-cloths. The table is crammed full: crockery bowls spilling over with mashed potatoes, gravy, and stuffing; pumpkin pies in each corner; two large roasted turkeys on metal trays.

The actors don't have plates. Instead, as the food is passed around the table, they sample it with their own spoons and forks. Everyone nods and smiles, taking small bites, politely handing the bowls along.

Ruth laughs quietly at the ridiculousness of the elabo-rate set-up. But a familiar shimmer of heat spreads across the back of her scalp, and without thinking too much about it, she picks one of the characters to follow along with. In this case, it's a woman at the far end of the table with a gray bonnet pulled tight over her head. Ruth begins matching the woman's spoonfuls with short gulps from her soup.

It doesn't take long for the feast to spin out of control. One of the men plants his face in a pie and slurps up the filling. Another rips a leg off one of the turkeys. He clamps his teeth into it and tears away the flesh before ripping off a second leg. The bonneted woman rapid-fires her spoon from the serving bowls to her mouth until she's wearing a beard of dressing and potatoes.

Ruth sways lightly, imagining the whole world caught up in this kind of frenzy, savoring the explosion of flavor as the soup runs down her throat. As soon as she polishes it off, she wolfs down the first slice of pizza before reaching for the second one and, minutes later, the third. All thoughts of her own worries and responsibilities, of Christopher and Daniel, are completely blotted out as she stuffs the food into her mouth and stares at the screen.

The video ends with the woman and two of the men guzzling cranberry sauce and then all of the actors circling a nearby trash barrel. Any food that hasn't been consumed is smeared across their faces and down the fronts of their costumes. Satisfied, nearly full, Ruth switches the channel. She wants to end her glut with something more romantic—a young Italian couple lying in a summer meadow, perhaps, sipping Chianti and feeding each other from a plate of linguini.

She clicks the button several times, teasing herself with nibbles from her first donut, but turns when she hears shouts coming from the main room. Peering through the grate at the top of the stall door, she sees the young man from downstairs. He's leaning across the pink desk, his chef's hat deflated and flopping over. The woman in the housedress is slumped in her chair, grinning.

The man wants to know what's so goddam fucking funny. Wants to know why the woman is sitting on her fat ass when she could be cleaning or helping out downstairs. There's only one customer, for chrissakes! The woman grabs his wrist, saying it's not nice for him to talk to his mother that way. She laughs when he shakes his arm free, points his finger in her face, and continues his tirade.

As Ruth watches them fight and listens to the young man's angry obscenities, all the pleasure and excitement she's been feeling drains out of her. She glances at her half-eaten donut. Its thick, yellow-custard filling has begun oozing onto her thumb, and she drops it into the wastebasket. She wipes her hand with a napkin and turns to get rid of the other donut, planning to leave just as soon as the man goes back downstairs.

Another outdoor scene is playing on the television now, the camera zooming in on a table set for a child's birthday party. Plates stacked with cookies and brownies. A long sheet cake divided into squares.

Ruth can't understand how a family's video diary could end up at a glut hut. Disgusted, she reaches for the channel button, but stops short as a flock of children descend on the table. They push and elbow in from every direction, gobbling the food as fast as they can, a blur of brown skin and black hair. Only after the table is cleared can Ruth make out the individual kids: hollow-eyed little boys and girls with bloated tummies and bony, concentration-camp arms and legs. They stagger away across a dirt field as a tall white man threatens them with a stick and then turns smiling into the camera.

How could anyone use poor starving children like this? What sorts of freaks get their jollies watching something so disturbing?

Ruth pictures Daniel, beautiful and innocent, waving to her from his car seat. She shuts her eyes, covers her ears, and tells herself to keep calm. What was she thinking coming to this sick, horrible place?

The young man is still yelling at his mother, but Ruth can't wait any longer. She puts on her sunglasses and opens the stall door. The man and woman don't notice her until she's halfway across the room, beelining for the stairs. He asks if everything is okay. Ruth keeps her chin tucked into her chest and hurries by without answering.

Outside it's pouring rain. Ruth is drenched even before she makes it to the grass median next to the restaurant parking lot. Her stomach groans as she reaches the dumpster. She leans against it, coughing and taking in desperate gulps of air. Only after she's convinced that she's not going to be sick does she jog the last few yards to her car.

Hunched over, fumbling for her keys, she hears someone calling her name. A woman's voice. Ruth doesn't want to find out who it could be. She gets into the car, dripping water everywhere, and jams the key into the ignition. The engine is barely in gear before she steps on the gas and pulls away. In the rearview mirror, she sees a figure behind her, standing in the parking lot waving, gray and unrecognizable in the rain. A friend of hers leaving the restaurant? She'll simply have to say she didn't notice if the person confronts her. And if the person saw her leaving the glut hut? Ruth knows that's a question she can't consider at the moment, and she swallows the panic rising in her throat. She steers into the Lee-Jackson traffic, wipers flapping, and focuses all of her attention on the road.

Half a mile along, there's a backup. Red and blue emergency lights flash ahead. Ruth leans to one side and sees a police cruiser on the shoulder and a tow truck blocking the right lane. She squeezes the steering wheel, still breathing hard, still coughing. After several minutes, the traffic refusing to budge, she pulls the wheel hard to the left, makes a U-turn, and steers onto a side street.

Two quick rights and a long straightaway. Ruth knows these roads well, but avoids them. She makes sure not to look over when she passes the tiny house she lived in with her mother until, when she was twelve, her mother died. For the six years that followed, Ruth was placed in a series of foster homes.

But then it's all behind her: She's crossed the county line and is soon climbing into the hills near her house, evergreen woods closing in around her like a welcome home. By the time she's cruising along Puddle Duck Hiway, breathing easier, the rain has died down. After turning off the wipers, she reaches into the glove compartment for the plastic box of Tic-Tacs she keeps there. She finds it, pops three of the tiny mints into her mouth, and sucks on them for a few seconds before crunching them to bits.

She manages a smile. Tonight will be a hot soak in the Jacuzzi, a glass or three of Chardonnay, a cathartic sorry-for-herself cry. She'll pull herself together before the guys come home tomorrow.

As she turns into the driveway, though, she sees Christopher's Lexus parked in front of the house, its metallic finish winking in the sun that's come out again. What's happened? Is Daniel all right? She pulls up close behind the Lexus, cuts the engine on her own car, and hurries inside. Before she can call out to Christopher, his voice comes from the kitchen, echoing through the great room and the main entrance hall, telling her that they just got here, that Dad wasn't feeling too good.

Ruth stands rooted to the floor, her clothes damp and chill against her goose-pimpled skin. She knows she should run upstairs and change, should come up with an excuse for where she's been. Instead, she finds herself walking the series of hallways to the back of the house.

Daniel is sitting on the edge of one of the big islands, his plump legs dangling. He watches his father slicing an apple into thin wedges. They both glance up smiling when Ruth enters the room, Daniel calling Mommy, Christopher explaining that he hasn't had time to put a proper lunch together. Cocking his head, he points out that she must have gotten caught in the downpour.

She starts to say something, but Christopher isn't looking for an answer. He's back to slicing the apple, telling her how worried he is about his father, how unfair it seems: It's been only eighteen months since his dad retired as dean of the prestigious Cutler prep school in town—and most difficult to accept, less than a year since his mother passed away. Daniel is pouting, saying Granddaddy sick.

Ruth nods at her son, her eyes filling with tears. Not for the first time, it occurs to her how little she grew up with, how Christopher—her wonderful "younger man"—gave her everything, and how, still, she has to have more, more, more. The glut hut comes to mind, and it's now this thought she pushes away, vowing to herself that she'll never visit one again. It's a promise she's made dozens of times, but this time is different: At this moment, she's positive, almost completely certain, that she really means it.

She gives Daniel a nuzzle and Christopher a peck on the cheek, apologizing for how hungry, how *starving*, her poor guys must be, telling them both to sit down at the table. Mommy's home now, she says, and before she does absolutely anything else, she's going to fix them something good to eat.

Truth

PAUL STOREY, IAN DRINKWATER,

AND NEW FRIENDS

1974

School lets out the first Friday of June. It's the end of sixth grade at last, the end of our time at Clifford J. Lewis Elementary. Ian Drinkwater and I walk home together, along the orange-dirt path behind the hospital as usual, not yet worried about junior high and the new paths home we'll need to learn, excited only about the long summer ahead. By the time we reach his house, the two of us have our plans all mapped out, plans that begin with meeting up with Wilson and Eddie the next day: the Four Fuckers on the loose for the next three months!

At breakfast on Saturday, though, my father reminds the family that our grandmother is driving up from Greenville for a visit. He's finishing his coffee, and he looks into his cup for a moment before looking at me, his rimless glasses magnifying his deep-set hazel eyes. "She'll be here by lunchtime," he says. "The mower is gassed up and ready to go.

I expect you to have your lawn work done before she arrives." He's recently added cutting the grass and weeding under the holly bushes to my list of jobs.

My father is stick thin and very tall. After getting up from the table, he ducks toward me to avoid the ceiling fan inches above his head. "And I mean well before she arrives," he says, before sucking air between his teeth. It's a wet, backward whistle I used to find funny. These days, he makes the sound mainly when he's brooding about something or is unhappy with me. I don't protest, just stare at my plate, poking a fork at my Eggo chunks drowning in syrup.

But then he leaves for some meeting at church, and before I can even start on the yard, my mother is pressing a dollar bill into my hand. She's forgotten to buy milk and needs me to go pick up a half-gallon at the A&P on Winchester Boulevard.

This is my chance to hang out with the gang for a while. I figure, what's the difference whether the trip to the store takes fifteen minutes or sixty? Even if my father returns home while I'm gone and sees that I haven't done any work yet, I can say I was simply running the errand I'd been told to run. He'll probably bark at me, demanding to know what took so long, but I'm willing to risk it.

So I head up the sidewalk toward Ian's, a bright morning sun hovering above Mount Warren and already feeling toasty on my shoulders and the backs of my legs. The outfit I've thrown on is my favorite: cutoff shorts, my black Converse All-Stars, and the Rolling Stones T-shirt I bought at the Record Zone, with the red lips-and-tongue logo spilling down the front. I used the money my grandmother gave me at Easter to buy it, thinking I'd show it off at school. My father said absolutely not, but my mother convinced him to at least let me wear it around the house and on weekends.

❖

My father seemed to be angry with me all the time that year, with trivialities—or at least what I thought should have been easily resolved matters—setting him off constantly. I'd leave a glass on the living room coffee table and he'd shout at me for being a dimwit, trying to ruin the furniture with a water stain. My cluttered bedroom was no longer a mess that needed straightening before bedtime; it was the "god-dam'dest pigsty" he'd ever seen in his life. If I left a book or magazine on my floor, he'd threaten to light a bonfire with anything I didn't put away properly. He had no interest in resolving anything easily or peacefully with me.

My mother didn't interfere during his blow-ups, but at least she would try to smooth things over later, asking me about school and teachers and friends. My father, on the other hand, would announce new chores that I was to do around the house. Some were akin to what other boys my age were expected to do, like loading the sharp-edged metal garbage barrels in back of the house and making sure they got to the street on time for pickup. Most, though, seemed designed to teach me a lesson—cleaning the bathroom floor on my hands and knees, for instance, and scrubbing between the tiles with an old toothbrush.

Never satisfied, my father would simmer and stew until his next blow-up. Maybe he was beginning to notice something in me that bothered the hell out of him, something he feared or knew he could never love. I don't know.

✢

Our subdivision is a network of dead-end streets and cul-de-sacs, dozens of Circles, Terraces, and Ways that spider-web down the side of a big wooded hill in the north part of Brookford. Ian's house is at the top. White brick, with rust-colored shutters and a second-floor balcony that faces the street, it's the first thing anyone sees when they turn into the neighborhood from busy Winchester Boulevard. Because my house is just two streets away, I can hike to Ian's in four minutes flat.

The place looks deserted when I get there, but as I step up to the back door, I hear music rumbling from inside the house, what sounds like a top-40-radio song—"Crocodile Rock" or "Bad, Bad Leroy Brown." I have to knock several times before Ian finally answers the door, still in his pajamas and a fuzzy yellow robe that looks too small for him. He tells me that his parents and brother are out of town for the day. His sister, Samantha, who's two years ahead of us in school, has invited friends over.

"They're using the *good* stereo," he says, rolling his eyes. "We can go listen to music upstairs if you want."

"I thought we were gonna get together with Wilson and Eddie at the fort."

"No, Wilson had to go somewhere with his dad, and I already tried Eddie's house twice and no one picked up the phone." He adjusts his large glasses on the bridge of his nose.

Explaining that I can't stay long—disappointed that our meet-up with the gang isn't going to happen after all—I follow Ian through the kitchen, the air thick with the smell of buttered popcorn. As we start up the front stairs, Samantha calls from the living room, "Hey, Ian, you and Paul wanna play Truth or Dare?"

⁘

Initially, the worst for my father was that I'd started to lose my interest in sports and instead had taken to rock music with an obsessive passion. I'd always been the kind of kid who'd race home from school and shoot hoops in the driveway until it got dark, refusing to go inside until I'd sunk fifty baskets from the free-throw line I'd drawn with colored chalk. Every autumn since I could remember, my father and I would linger after church each Sunday with the other fathers and sons, talking the talk about football in general and our Redskins in particular. On Sunday afternoons, he and I would set up in front of the TV, hollering at it, calling for my mother to bring us more chip 'n' dip and Coke. She'd keep my little brother and sister out of the way so we could enjoy our game together. Whenever the Redskins scored—and they scored a lot in those days—we'd whoop and cheer and fake wrestle on the couch, usually until he'd cheat and start poking my ribs with his knuckles. Or we'd reenact whatever gravity-defying play we'd just witnessed on the screen that had put points on the board for the Skins. After a while, though, we'd turn back to watching the game. "That could be you some day," he said once, after one of our wrestling matches. He pointed at one of the players on the screen, dead serious. "I mean it, Paul."

During halftime breaks, throwing football in the backyard together, I'd do my best to pass a perfect spiral each time, delivering the ball right into my father's hands. He rarely had to take more than a single step in any direction. I started to believe what he had said, or at least had implied: that I, Paul Storey, average kid from average small-town Brookford, could go anywhere I wanted to go.

But then, early in that sixth-grade year, I discovered the Rolling Stones—and I began to rethink what "anywhere" might be. Ian's big brother had gone off to college and left a pile of records behind, including a live album by the Stones called *Get Yer Ya-Ya's Out!* Ian had me to his house for a sleepover in his attic, and on his pack-it-up stereo, we listened to Mick Jagger belt out "Jumpin' Jack Flash" and then tease the crowd, telling them he'd lost a button on his pants and was afraid they might drop: "You don't want my trousers to fall down, now *do* ya?"

Ian, propped up on one elbow next to the record player, moved the needle back to the beginning of the song each time it ended so that we could listen to it again and again and again. I lay staring up at the cotton-candy insulation stuffed between the exposed roof beams. I imagined I was inside an immense cathedral, jumping and prancing around like Mick while the music echoed off the pink-stone walls and stained-glass windows above me.

Later, after we switched off the stereo and the lights, Ian scooted close to me. He unzipped my sleeping bag and slid his hand beneath the waistband of my pajama bottoms. "What if Karen Markowitz was doing this to you right now?" he whispered as he rubbed me between the legs.

We'd groped each other before, both of us saying how fantastic it would be if Karen—or Beth Garrow or Mary-anne Stalling—were there touching us like that, but that night I grabbed his hand away. "I'm not a homo, Ian. Don't do that anymore."

Except for those rare occasions when Ian and I have been allowed to play records on the "good" stereo, the Drink-waters' formal living room, with its expensive but uncom-fortable-looking furniture, has always been off-limits to kids. So it's strange seeing it taken over by Samantha and her friends. Samantha herself—sweet-faced, and pudgy like Ian—is lounging on the pineapple-print sofa with a massive bowl of popcorn in her lap, her dirty bare feet propped on the coffee table in front of her. Next to her, also barefooted, and trying to fish an ice cube out of a tall drinking glass, sits Cassie Maybaugh, a thin girl with white-blonde hair who I've seen a lot when hanging out at Ian's. Both girls wear denim skirts and sherbet-colored halter tops.

"Hey, Paul," Samantha says. "You know Cassie, right?"

"*Sam,* of *course* he knows me," Cassie says, giving up on the ice. "He's over here all the time." She squints at me, tilting her head as if a weight has been attached to one of her ears.

I say hi to the girls. My attention, though, is drawn to Samantha's other friend, who's kneeling on the floor, flipping through a stack of albums next to the stereo console. Samantha says, "Oh, that's Zack," but I already recognize Zack Bloomgarden, a ninth-grader whose mother teaches the special ed class at my school. I've never actually met him, but he's infamous around town for having the longest hair anyone has ever seen a guy wear, other than rock stars on album covers. Chocolate brown, parted in the middle, and tucked behind his ears, it pours down his back, ending in a straight-edged cut two inches below his waist.

"Nice shirt," he says, turning toward me. "You like the Stones?" The shirt he wears—a baseball jersey with gold three-quarter sleeves—is stenciled with a giant Superman "S."

"They're my favorite group."

"Cool."

As he stands up, he raises his eyebrows as though genuinely glad to be having a conversation with me, which makes me a little uncomfortable. I put my hands in my pockets and go over to the albums. They're the ones Ian and I have been listening to. I thumb through them until I find *Get Yer Ya-Ya's Out!* and hold it up for Zack. "This one's pretty good."

"All right, man, let's put it on." He takes the record out

of the sleeve and lowers it onto the turntable, his forearms disappearing inside the mammoth walnut console. "Much better than this crap," he says, and switches one of the console's knobs, cutting off "Tie a Yellow Ribbon" in mid verse.

"I *like* that song," Cassie says from her seat on the couch, as the record hisses and crackles.

Zack catches my eye and grins. "Well, we like *this* song."

I pretend to study the album cover while the first chords of "Jumpin' Jack Flash" blast through the speakers. When Mick wails, "I was *born* in a cross-fire hurricane," Zack cranks the volume and spins away from me. He hooks his thumbs into his armpits and juts his chin out and back like a chicken.

All of his dancing around makes the record skip occasionally, and Samantha yells at him to be careful. Normally I'd be annoyed too, but I'm busy gazing at his hippie hair and the way he wiggles his butt beneath his patched and faded hippie jeans. When I glance over at Ian, he's slouched in a chair beside the doorway, frowning at me, so I look away and keep my eyes on Zack.

✢✢✢

Having someone else's warm hands on me had been such a huge thrill the first couple of times, but I didn't like the guilt and anxiety that followed. How could I tell Ian that it wasn't the girls in our class I was thinking about? It wasn't any particular boy either, not even Ian who, although he was my best friend, sometimes reminded me of my great aunt

Sally: short and tubby, with thick, owl-like glasses that were always slipping down his nose.

No, what I felt mostly was a vague yearning for this romantic image I'd conjured up. Had I dreamt it? Or created it from something I'd seen on TV? Me, heading off to battle with a ragged band of young men, then celebrating our victory, arms draped over one another's shoulders, all of us swigging black ale from heavy pewter tankards and weeping like we'd never wept before for those among us who hadn't survived. I'm sure this fantasy was tangled up in my love of sports. Rooting for my teams—the Redskins, the Bullets, the Orioles—and tacking up pictures of my favorite players felt perfectly natural, especially since my father loved sports too. But I had to admit to myself that it was also exciting in a way that I barely understood and knew I could never explain to him.

Hanging out with my neighborhood friends gave me a similar feeling. Ian, Wilson Hopewell, Eddie Carter, and I started a secret gang we called the 4-F Club—the Four Fuckers. When we weren't shooting hoops, we were meeting in the woods behind Wilson's house, at the fort we'd built from pine branches. We cussed, hawked loogies, occasionally passed around a cigarette if we were able to swipe one from our parents, all the while plotting undercover raids on the neighborhood. We never did anything other than steal a stack of antique license plates from elderly Mrs. Thompson's garage, but being with those boys—being a member of that club—was a thrill I tried to hide from my parents. Any time they asked who I'd been running around with on a weekend afternoon, I'd lie and say no one if I thought I could get away with it. I told myself I was protecting the secrecy of the gang, when the truth was I didn't want my parents noticing any sign of excitement on my part—a certain look in my eyes or a giveaway reddening of my cheeks. I was afraid of them telling me it was wrong.

But lying in the dark at Ian's, with "Jumpin' Jack Flash" and the vision of a humping, pumping Mick Jagger still ping-ponging around in my head—*that* was excitement unlike anything I'd known before, and I didn't care if it was wrong. Within days I was begging my mother for an electric guitar for Christmas, strutting in front of her full-length mirror imagining my hair down to my shoulders, sneaking my father's reel-to-reel tape recorder from the spare bedroom closet to hear myself imitate Mick.

‑{∙}‑

As soon as "Jumpin' Jack Flash" is over, Samantha says enough, time for Truth or Dare. I wish I could spend the rest of the morning listening to the album with Zack, but he turns down the stereo. "Yes, ma'am," he says, and makes an elaborate show of clicking his heels and saluting her before squeezing next to her on the sofa. I take a seat on the Oriental rug in front of the coffee table, my legs crossed Indian-style. I've never played the game before. I figure I'll just follow everyone else's lead.

After announcing that she'll go first—"My house, my rules"—Samantha notices that Ian hasn't budged from his seat by the doorway. "Let's *go*," she says, and waits while he shuffles across the room and plops down on the floor next to me. She glares at him before speaking to Cassie on her left. "The circle goes this way. We play the way we did that day Ruth came over, okay? The first person asks a question, then the other person either answers truthfully"—she eyes each of us, wagging her finger—"or they have to do a dare."

Cassie nods. Zack says, "Oh yeah, that day Ruth came over. That makes sense." He shoots me a what-the-hell look. I bite the inside of my cheek, forcing myself not to laugh.

Samantha ignores him and turns to Cassie again. "I get to ask you first. So, let's see . . ." She peers up at the ceiling, drumming her fingers on her chin. "Okay, I've got one: How many guys have you gone to third base with?"

Cassie's face goes red. "Exactly *none,* for your information," she says.

"But I thought—"

"*No,*" Cassie says. She stares at Samantha until Samantha finally lowers her eyes and says, "All *right*, don't be so touchy. I thought you wanted to play."

Cassie shrugs. "I *do*. I guess I just like asking better than answering, that's all."

Zack laughs out loud. "We *noticed*."

"Just take a fucking dare next time," Samantha says.

Cassie sticks her tongue out at both of them before focusing her attention on me. "*Any*-way, *my* turn now." She folds her hands in her lap and adjusts herself in her seat until she's sitting up perfectly straight. "So, Paul . . . hmm

. . . If you could make out with anyone in this room, who would it be?"

I'm still debating with myself whether or not I know what third base is. Now I wonder if Cassie means who I'd kiss or who I'd want to fool around with. Without thinking, I glance at Zack.

"Hey, man, don't look at me," he says.

I turn back to Cassie. "Uh, *you*, I guess." She grins.

Samantha buries her face in her hands and pretends to sob. She keeps this up for a good while—to the point where I begin to think she might really be upset—but then, snickering, lets her hands fall. Before she can call on me, though, Ian says, "This is dumb. I'm not playing." He pushes himself up from the floor. "Let's go upstairs," he says to me.

"Paul can stay with us if he wants," Samantha says. "If you don't wanna play, go do something else—and change out of your PJs and that dippy robe already. You look like Retardo Man or something."

"Shut up, butthole," Ian says. "Come on, Paul."

I want to keep playing and don't say anything. I hear him breathing through his mouth behind me, but he doesn't wait for me to respond before leaving the room. "Thanks a lot," he says, and marches up the stairs.

"What's *his* problem?" Cassie says.

Samantha grabs a handful of popcorn. "Forget him. He's such a stupid little pinhead sometimes."

I look over my shoulder, thinking maybe I should follow Ian after all, regretting that I've ignored him. But when Samantha calls my name, I try my best not to worry about it.

"Go," she says. "It's your turn to ask Zack."

I want to think of something good, something that will impress these older kids, but with Cassie whining "Come on," I end up asking Zack the same question she asked me: "Who would *you* make out with in this room."

Zack looks the girls over. "Can I make out with both of 'em?"

Cassie reaches across Samantha's lap and smacks Zack's leg. "You are so *bad.*"

I wonder what would happen if he were to pick me but can't imagine what I'd do if he actually pointed at me and took a step in my direction. The thought puts my stomach in my throat.

He shakes his head. "I can't choose, man. I'll have to take a dare."

Everyone looks at me, but I have no idea what to suggest.

"Make him go streaking," Samantha says.

Cassie's eyes get big. "*Yeah,* make him streak to the sidewalk and back."

"Hold it," Zack says, "I'm not running outside buck-ass naked."

Cassie starts to say something, but he puts his hand up. "Wait." He sits thinking for a few moments, then says, "All right, I got it. Y'all go outside in front and watch."

"No, we get to pick the dare," Samantha says.

"If you don't like it, I'll do something else," he says as he gets up from the sofa. "Okay?" He slides his hands into his pockets and rocks back on his heels. "Go on."

The girls and I hurry out the front door to the manicured hedge bordering the sidewalk. After a couple of minutes, Zack steps out onto the second-floor balcony wearing a fancy maroon dress with short puffed sleeves and a white lace collar. He does a slow twirl, then begins waving and blowing kisses, like a parade queen riding in the back of a convertible. "How do you like it?" he calls.

"*Gor*-geous!" Cassie calls back.

Samantha is laughing, but she tries to be serious. "If you ruin my mother's dress—"

"Don't worry," Zack says, "I'll take it off right now." He bends over so we can't see him, then leaps up, flashing his long bare back and naked white ass as his hair flies above his shoulders.

The girls are laughing hysterically and clapping their hands. My heart is pumping as fast as it ever has in my life. I stand there, frozen in place, until I notice that the girls have gone back inside without me, and I run to catch up with them. A minute later, Zack saunters down the stairs in his regular clothes, winding his hair behind his ears, a huge grin plastered across his face. The girls are saying, "Oh my *God*" and "Let's keep going."

Samantha brings a pitcher of pink lemonade and a box of Oreos from the kitchen as the four of us gather at the coffee table again. The room gets hot and stuffy as the temperature climbs outside, but no one cares as we go around and around the circle. I barely notice the back door slamming when Ian leaves the house.

❖

My father didn't know about Ian and me fooling around; didn't know that I hid his copies of *Sports Illustrated* under my pillow so I could pore over the close-up photos of the hard, glistening bodies with my flashlight at night; didn't know about the Four Fuckers; didn't know that I feared him taking me over his knee if he ever found out about any of this.

But he did know that my new interest in rock "concerned" him, as he put it. And at first, early that year, before his angry outbursts became part of his everyday routine, he thought he could talk me out of it.

"That music and those awful people," he said, with a gesture toward the doorway, as if referring to the entire world. "It's the worst kind of decadence, Paul." He'd poured us each a glass of my mother's sweet tea in the kitchen and led me into the den for a chat. "Do you know what that means, 'decadence'?"

Sitting on the room's small sofa, I told him I didn't.

"Decay and death, that's as good a definition as any." He held my gaze, leaning forward from his armchair and resting his elbows on his knees, which pointed up so high they were practically level with my shoulders.

Not knowing what to say, I took a sip of my tea. Outside,

my little brother and the Everett twins from next door were playing on the jungle gym in our side yard. I could hear their giggly laughter and their high-pitched shouts to one another. My father sighed at my silence. Backward-whistling through his teeth, he stood and went to the window, where he parted the curtains slightly and peered out at them.

"All these hippies and freaks and fairies," he said. "They think only of themselves, and they think they know better than God Himself."

"But you and Mom liked the Beatles, didn't you?" I said, remembering the story they told of bringing me with them to the drive-in to see *A Hard Day's Night* when I was a toddler.

"Things were completely different then, son, before the dope and the crazies and all. This is serious now. You know that. Your cousin Tom Laney has just about killed Aunt Jean and Uncle Ron, first when he up and quit basketball, and now with his girly long hair and marijuana smoking and all the problems it's caused. Is that something you want to get caught up in and put us through?"

"No, sir."

He nodded toward the window. "Is that what you want for your brother?"

"No."

"Because he looks up to you, you know."

"Yes, sir."

"Good, then."

"But . . . I just like the music," I said. "I don't care about the other stuff."

My father let go of the curtain and looked at me again. "It all goes hand in hand these days, Paul. Trust me on this."

I did trust him on that: I knew it went hand in hand. I didn't just like the music, I liked it all—Mick's obscene lips, Alice Cooper's eye makeup dripping down his cheeks like black candle wax, David Bowie's bright orange shag-cut and his earrings and boas and sequin-covered jumpsuits. I loved it, but I couldn't tell my father. He wouldn't understand. And I didn't believe anything *he'd* said. Death? Decay? As far as I was concerned, this was as good as life got.

⋅⊹⋅

Zack and Samantha don't have as much of a problem being honest as Cassie does. Even so, eventually each of us has to "do a dare." Zack puts on a dress again—this time a sleeveless blue one of Samantha's with a violet silk bow on each shoulder—and struts up and down the sidewalk in front of the house until a car drives by. Samantha has to sit on the balcony in her bra and panties, which is disappointing because the balcony's railing all but hides her completely. Cassie refuses several dares until finally agreeing to call one of her teachers at home. She's supposed to ask for Mr. Goodlaw and then breathe heavily into the receiver when he comes to the phone. But she chickens out. When Mr. Goodlaw's wife answers, she says, "Sorry, wrong number" and hangs up.

Then my turn comes. Cassie has been lobbing fairly easy

questions my way—"Have you ever kissed a girl before?" "When's the last time you cried?"—until she says, "What's the *weirdest* thing you ever did?"

I scramble to invent something that will let me off the hook, but my mind starts racing. I can't help it. I picture Ian and me in our sleeping bags touching each other, and me under the covers with my father's sports magazines. My mouth goes dry; my cheeks burn red hot.

Zack says, "Man, your face has *dare* written all over it."

That's all it takes for the three of them to pounce, the girls each grabbing an arm and pulling me up from the floor, Zack gripping my shoulders from behind. They steer me up the stairs and into Samantha's room, where they force me onto her soft canopy bed.

My father didn't hit me, though there were times that year when he probably wanted to. He'd done that only once, when I was seven. My sister was a baby, and I'd called to my parents downstairs, screaming that she'd fallen out of her bedroom window, thinking what a great joke. But when they came running up the back steps from the kitchen, sounding like a thunderstorm headed my way, I knew I was in for it. They flew into the room, my father's face as white as milk, my mother wild-eyed until she saw my sister safe in her crib. They turned on me with such fury that I burst into terrified sobs, but that didn't stop my father from dragging me down the hall and into their room. He yanked my pants down and whaled away on my butt and the backs of my legs. As I wriggled to get loose, crying and begging him to stop, I saw my mother standing in the hall just beyond the half-closed door, rocking my sister in her arms. My three-year-old brother sat at her feet sucking his thumb.

That night, my father came into my room after I'd gone to bed. I squeezed my eyes shut when the door creaked, but he could tell I wasn't asleep. He told me he took no pleasure in hurting me, but that I needed to know what a bad scare I'd given him and my mother.

"Playing dumb tricks like that is only going to get you into trouble," he said. "You're to tell us the truth, Paul. *Always.*"

Zack brings out the blue dress. I shoot up from the bed saying, "No way" but then let them push me down again, electricity buzzing along my spine at the thought of strutting around like Zack had. I pretend to resist, but soon they've slipped the dress over my head and zipped it in back. Zack gets two handfuls of toilet paper from the bathroom and stuffs it down the front. Cassie squeezes my cheeks to make me pucker, and Samantha blots red lipstick all over my mouth. They brush on rouge and green eyeshadow as I squinch up my face.

Through the late winter and on into spring, little by little, my father gave up trying to have chats with me about rock music and how concerned he was. He'd make the occasional comment about freaks and fairies, but he must have realized that he couldn't very well forbid me from listening to rock altogether. It was everywhere—on the radio, at the Record Zone that had recently opened, on the albums at my friends' houses.

Maybe he thought I'd come to see things his way or, if not, at least start getting excited about sports again, something we'd shared since I was little. But I didn't do either. So he yelled at me and stomped around mad and piled on the chores. If he'd begun to convince himself that my obsession with rock was truly poisoning me, twisting me into something I wouldn't have turned into otherwise, he might have figured that this was the only way to set me straight.

When they're done, Zack whistles. "Oh yeah, take a look." He points to Samantha's open closet, and I catch myself in the full-length mirror on the back of the door.

My tennis shoes look out of place and the dress is slightly baggy on me, but everything else has come together perfectly. The toilet paper fills out my chest. The blue background of my Stones shirt is a seamless match to the blue of the dress, and the logo is hidden from sight. The makeup narrows my cheeks and makes my lips and eyes explode with color.

"That is *unbelievable*," Samantha says.

I turn to see the three of them staring at me open-jawed.

Zack says, "Damn, *I'd* take you on a date," and right then, something—some unfamiliar feeling of relief or release—comes over me. I glance in the mirror again, determined to remember every detail of what's happening to me, before allowing my new friends to lead me downstairs and outside, where we walk out to the hedge and start along the sidewalk.

⸙

My father intercepted us before we'd made it even ten yards down the street. How did I not see him coming? Had he crossed over from the other side, or had a tree or telephone pole blocked him from view as he marched toward us? He seemed to just appear, and he stopped us cold.

"What the hell are you doing?" he said, staring at the dress, his voice tight with a choked-down rage that even in his angriest moments I'd never heard before.

"We're just having fun," Cassie said. But my father didn't want an answer from anyone other than me, and I didn't have one I could give him.

He loomed over us, half a foot taller even than Zack, his eyes moving slowly from my toilet-paper breasts to my painted face to the pink hair band Cassie had stuck on my head as we left Samantha's room. I could practically feel the heat of his anger as he stood there drawing wind between his teeth, making that high whistling sound I'd come to dread.

To this day, I'm certain that he was two seconds away from dragging me home and giving me the whipping he'd wanted to give me for months.

But suddenly the storm broke—the air around us seemed to loosen—and my father was speaking to the space above my head in a quiet voice. "Go change and come on home now. Mamaw's going to be here soon." He turned away, then glanced back, still not looking me in the eye. I don't think he ever looked me in the eye again.

"Did you get the milk for your mother?" he said.

"No, sir, I can go—"

"Doesn't matter, just come on home."

It took me fifteen minutes to change out of the dress and clean my face with soap and hot water, rubbing my cheeks until they were raw, dabbing at the skin around my eyes until it burned. Zack, Samantha, and Cassie stayed out of my way in the living room, and I left the house without saying anything to them.

Ian, who was my best friend then, has remained one of my closest and most loyal friends over the years—even after he stayed in Brookford while I left for New York, having discovered late in high school a passion for writing, which I came to realize was stronger than my adolescent love of rock music could ever be. Nevertheless, best friend or not, Ian was upset with me that day. He told me later that he met up with Wilson Hopewell after all. They wandered by my house, and my father asked if they'd seen me. Hoping to get me into trouble, Ian said yes, explaining that his parents were away and that I was alone with his sister, another ninth-grade girl, and a hippie-looking guy he didn't know that well. "They were playing some weird game," he told my father. "The guy had my mom's dress on."

⁌⁐

I hurry home, but the lawnmower isn't in the garage: Its slot next to the workbench is empty. As I stand there catching my breath, the engine fires up outside. I go around to the side of the garage and see that my father has started on the backyard. He's just made a turn and is walking away from me, pushing the mower toward the gravel alley that runs behind our house. I yell for him to stop, shouting that I can help, that this is *my* job. He pauses, his shoulders stiffen, but then he continues on, as if the sound of the engine is too loud and he can't hear me above the noise.

Great to Meet You!

PAUL PURSUED

2000

From: Timothy Waters <waterfall@u-bettcha.com>
Sent: Friday, October 06, 11:32 PM
To: Paul Storey
Subject: Great to meet you!
Attachments: Windmills.doc; BigBook.doc

Hi, Paul,
Just dropping you a quick line to tell you how pleased
I was to meet you tonight—a fellow "struggling artist"!
I'm sorry we didn't get to talk more. It would've been fun
to bar-hop and chat into the wee hours. Oh well, another
time, right?

I have to say that these guest-speaker events are usually
so unfulfilling, for me at least. I show up with notebook
in hand, ready to jot down pointers from the "masters"—

like pinching crumbs off the kitchen floor, I guess—but inevitably, I come away disappointed. After their readings, the "esteemed" authors (can't the event planners think up another adjective?) either go on and on about their brilliant careers and their ever-supportive spouses and children, or any advice they offer is so vague or esoteric. (Like tonight, when Dr. Stewart mentioned "the art of suffering and suffering for your art." What does that mean?!)

And then, to make it worse, the crowd always act like such sycophants. Didn't you hate how everyone laughed just a <u>little</u> too loudly at Dr. Stewart's jokes when he came into the reception hall and then pressed ahead to get close to him? I've never seen so many martini and wine glasses balanced in the air as everybody tried to slip forward through the throng!

Paul, if you don't mind me saying so, I could tell right away that you were different. When I spied you across the room at the drinks table—away from the sheep!—with your thumb hooked in the pocket of your jeans, sipping your whiskey (I believe you said you're a Scotch man, no?), my first thought was "Well now, <u>here</u> stands Mr. Down-to-Earth." And I mean that as a compliment! I just knew you'd be the kind who doesn't give two flips about what the "real" artists have to say. And you confirmed it for me with your interesting and original story concepts, as well as your unique "take" on life in gen-

eral—all in that wonderful Southern dialect of yours.
(By the by, I want to hear more about your "subway-as-id" philosophy!) <u>And</u>, to top it off, your recent publishing successes! Congratulations!! I called us struggling artists before, but you're much less a "struggler" than I! Three pieces in three journals in six months?! (Which ones were they again?) And your second novel coming out next year? Color me impressed! . . . and green with envy. Just kidding. :-) (As I told you, I'm still waiting for that first nibble, but it <u>will</u> happen!)

Anyway, Paul, I'm completely inspired after our all-too-brief conversation. I hope you don't mind that I've attached a couple of things here: my latest piece, "Windmills on Sixth Avenue," as well as the first few chapters of my own novel in progress (as yet untitled). I'd be interested to know what you think. And please send me some of your work. Can't wait to read anything you're willing to show me!

Again, Paul, very nice to meet you. All best wishes!
Tim W.

————————————————————————————————————

From: Timothy Waters <waterfall@u-bettcha.com>
Sent: Monday, October 09, 7:38 AM
To: Paul Storey
Subject: RE: Great to meet you!

Hi (again), Paul,

I had a little time before I dash off to work this morning and thought I'd check in to make sure you received my note from last week. (Maybe I don't have the right e-mail address?)

Anyway, if you have a minute and could shoot a mail my way, at least letting me know you're "out there," I'd appreciate it!

Best,
Tim Waters

——————————————————————————————————

From: Timothy Waters <waterfall@u-bettcha.com>
Sent: Wednesday, October 11, 9:44 PM
To: Paul Storey
Subject: RE: RE: Great to meet you!
Attachments: Windmills_REV.doc

Hello (again-again!), Paul,

I thought I'd give you one more try. I guess, though, I really must have the wrong address. :-(

In case you are there, I'm attaching a revision of "Windmills." I couldn't keep myself from picking at it! (Sigh.) But I'm sure you know what that's like. "Writing" is really "rewriting," as they say.

Please do let me know if you receive this mail.

Thanks,
Tim Waters

_____

From: Paul Storey <whatsyourstorey@ps-mail.com>
Sent: Friday, October 13, 3:16 PM
To: Timothy Waters

tim, got your posts, appreciate your interest.
in touch soon,
paul storey

_____

From: Timothy Waters <waterfall@u-bettcha.com>
Sent: Friday, October 13, 7:08 PM
To: Paul Storey
Subject: Thank you!

Hey, Paul,
Thanks for your e-mail!! I'm glad to know that I was actually "connecting," not just sending messages out into
the ether! :-)

As I said before, I hope you'll send me something of
yours to read. And I look forward to your comments on
my work, although I admit I'm a tad nervous! (Please

remember, too, to look at the <u>most</u> <u>recent</u> version of "Windmills." Thx!)

And hey, now that the weekend is upon us, is there a chance we could meet up? Maybe tomorrow, or even tonight for a late supper or nightcap? I'm free for whatever . . .

BTW, next Wednesday evening, Oliver Erickson is giving a reading at Beckett Books in the East Village (but I'm sure you knew that already). Are you planning to attend? Maybe afterwards we could grab a drink (or three???). Let me know.

All the best,
Tim

PS—I almost forgot (!): Although I didn't send you an updated file, please keep in mind, as you read the chapters from my novel, that I'm changing "Benjamin" to "Barney" throughout. The shorter name sounds better to me and gives the book a decidedly smoother flow. Also, in the "street scene" at the beginning of chapter 12, and then throughout most of chapters 15 and 16, I plan to refer to "lampposts" rather than "fire hydrants"—a more inspiring image, methinks! Anyway, not a big deal, but just so you know. Thx!

—————————————————————————————————————

From: Timothy Waters <waterfall@u-bettcha.com>
Sent: Tuesday, October 17, 6:21 PM
To: Paul Storey
Subject: RE: Thank you!
Attachments: Windmills_REV2.doc; BigBook_REV.doc

Hi, Paul,
I didn't hear back from you, so I figured you were all booked for the weekend. Hope you had a pleasant one. If I know you at all—and I suspect that I do!—you were hunched in front of your computer screen like I was! What else is new, eh?

Anyway, I'm e-mailing (again!) because I knew you'd appreciate this: A good friend of mine pointed out some inconsistencies in the revision of "Windmills on Sixth Avenue." (Thank God for those kinds of friends!) So, I am attaching to this mail yet another reworking of the story. Feel free to do what you will with the first two versions.

I also said to myself, "What the heck!" and decided to give you the updated version of my novel—with "Barney" and "lampposts" swapped in everywhere. It's attached, just so you'll have the correct version in front of you . . .

Lastly, you didn't let me know whether you're going to the Erickson reading tomorrow. Should I plan on meeting you there?

All the very best,
Tim

From: Paul Storey <whatsyourstorey@ps-mail.com>
Sent: Thursday, October 19, 3:23 PM
To: Timothy Waters

hi tim, not a big oliver erickson fan, sorry to say. also, i'm having trouble picturing you from the stewart event. were you the tall gentleman or the youngish man with red hair? when i wrote you before, i had you confused with someone else, somebody working on a screenplay he wanted me to read.

in fact, expecting the screenplay, i took a quick look at your windmills story. i enjoyed what i read, but the slap-stick involving the don quixote character soon became just a bit repetitive. I'd suggest cutting back on the comedy and expanding the rest of the piece.

hope this helps.

yours,
paul storey

From: Timothy Waters <waterfall@u-bettcha.com>
Sent: Thursday, October 19, 6:36 PM
To: Paul Storey

Subject: Thanks!
Attachments: Windmills_REV3.doc; AnEarlierIncident.
doc

Hi, Paul,

No, no, no, I walked up when you were talking to those two, remember? You shot me a look that said, "Rescue me, <u>please</u>!" (Believe me, I've been <u>there</u>.) No, I was the thin guy with the beard. Wearing the brown three-piece suit and the orange "power tie"? <u>Remember</u>?

Anyway, thanks for your mail (:-)) <u>and</u> for your comments on "Windmills." A few people in one of my writing groups originally suggested I pull back some of the "jokier" material too, and I did. But I wonder if you were reading the <u>very</u> latest version. (Remember, it was "REV2" not "REV" that I wanted you to look at.) Anyway, it doesn't matter; I've attached another revision to this e-mail ("REV3"). I guess I could just go on and on forever! Most of the humor is now stripped out <u>completely</u>. (And just so you know, I'm not at all married to the middle section—the part that begins "The lonely stretch of asphalt was now his chess board"—so skip over that if you feel the piece is stronger without it.)

Let me know what you think—if and when you're able to carve out some time in between your important work commitments.

DAVID LOTT

And I hope you don't mind, but I'm also attaching a <u>very</u> rough draft/detailed outline of a new story I put together in the last day or two—"An Earlier Incident." Yes, it's a parody—a takeoff on life in the city. I think I must have had your subway theory in mind when I wrote it. (Sorry if I filched!) I just love (<u>not</u>!) when I'm waiting for a train that's late, and they blare that inimitable, garbled announcement over the intercom, "After an earlier incident, please expect delays, blah, blah, blah." I'm always thinking track fire or "police action," but what if the actual "incident" is that the train conductor needs to make pit stops all along his route because he has a really bad hangover? (Or diarrhea?? Or <u>something</u>?!) I'm in my "brainstorming phase" right now, so I'm open to suggestions. (And FYI, please note that for easy reference, any time the conductor's "condition" is mentioned, I've put "H/D/O" in brackets—for "Hangover / Diarrhea / Other"—just a series of simple reminders until a final decision is reached.)

Anyway, I know it's a whimsical imagining, but I do hope at least that the humor in this new story doesn't seem too—or even a "bit"!—repetitive. ;-) But please be honest!

Best wishes,
Tim

PS—Sorry that you aren't an Oliver Erickson fan, and sorry that you missed what turned out to be an incredible evening at Beckett Books! I was not disappointed, as

I usually am. (Although, as with Dr. Stewart's reading, it was a fawn-fest after Mr. Erickson was done. I still can't get over how shameless a lot of these people are!) Oh well, let's shoot for another time and place. Can't wait!

————————————————————————————————

From: Timothy Waters <waterbug@a-ok.com>
Sent: Friday, October 20, 10:21 PM
To: Paul Storey
Subject: Tomorrow night?
Attachments: AnEarlierIncident_REV.doc

Hi, Paul,
Sorry to bug you. It's been one of those days, and I'm about three seconds from falling over—but I wanted to check in with you, for several reasons. First, I read back over "An Earlier Incident," and the hangover/diarrhea angle was simply not working. So I revised and revised and revised, and I now think I've got the piece where it needs to be. The updated version is attached. (It's still a bit over the top, with time travel and dream sequences throughout, but I have to admit it makes me laugh.)

Secondly, I'm writing to ask whether you'd want to get together tomorrow night—to catch up, share some ideas, etc. I'm on the Upper East Side (way East, off York), but could hop a train if you have a favorite watering hole somewhere. Let me know.

See you soon!
Tim

PS—Just so you know, I've switched Internet providers and my e-mail address is different now, as I'm sure you noticed. Please write me back at this new address going forward. (Sigh . . . It's always something, right?) Thx! :-)

––

From: Timothy Waters <waterbug@a-ok.com>
Sent: Saturday, October 21, 12:19 PM
To: Paul Storey
Subject: Tonight??
Attachments: Windmills_REV4.doc; AnEarlierIncident_REV2.doc; BigBookInsert_pg12.doc; BigBookInsert_pg 15.doc; BigBookInsert_pg23.doc; BigBookInsert_pg 36.doc; BigBookInsert_pg 58.doc; BigBookInsert_pg 77.doc; BigBookInsert_pg 87.doc; BigBookInsert_pg 103.doc

Hey, Paul,
Well, in the end, I couldn't sleep last night (after feeling so exhausted!). I tossed and turned, thinking about "Windmills" and "An Earlier Incident." Finally, I got out of bed and tore through revisions on each. I had no idea I could type that fast! I've attached the new versions. My changes made both pieces longer, but better. (I hope! . . . But let me know what you think.)

I've also attached various inserts to my novel, rather than bothering you with a completely new version. They are all coded to page numbers, so simply swap in each one when you reach its particular page. (This is better than a whole new file, right?)

BTW, I'm still up for going out tonight if you are. Drop me a line!

Best,
Tim

PS—By the way, Paul, consider yourself "Googled"! Since you haven't had a chance to send me any of your work yet, I thought I'd go find it myself. A couple of the journals that recently published your stories showed up in my search, so I'm planning to track them down. One of the sites mentioned that you've set some of your fiction in the small town you grew up in, Brookfield. (Or Brooktown?) So quaint! Anyway, I'm hoping to contact the editors. I might "mention your name" and submit something too. I don't usually like to pull strings, but you do what you've got to do, right? Oh, and your interview with that weekly arts paper (is that out of Chelsea?) was great! I loved your clown-story idea. Let me know where you are with that, because it's a super concept, and if you're not going to write the story, I will! (Just kidding :-))

From: Paul Storey <whatsyourstorey@ps-mail.com>
Sent: Saturday, October 21, 3:08 PM
To: Timothy Waters

tonight is out for me, tim. i'm traveling upstate for a conference.

i want to be clear, too, that i am stretched so thin these days with my own projects, i really don't have the time to devote myself to anything else. but best of luck to you.

paul storey

_____

From: Timothy Waters <waterbug@a-ok.com>
Sent: Sunday, October 22, 2:46 AM
To: Paul Storey
Subject: That is so weird . . .
Attachments: BigBook_REV2.doc; CCClown.doc

Paul,
That is so weird that after not hearing from you, I run into you (literally!) at Will o' the Wisp. What a fabulous bar! You mentioned it in that arts paper interview, and I just had to see it for myself.

Are you OK, by the way? I'm sorry I bounded out of the men's room like that! They should put up a sign: "Please Open Door Very Slowly; Otherwise, People on Other Side Will Get Smashed in the Face!" Sorry, bad joke. I guess

I'm still a little tipsy. And now I'm home and see that you <u>did</u> write back. (I didn't think to check my old address earlier. Remember, I have a <u>new</u> adress: waterbug@a-ok.com, <u>NOT</u> waterfall@u-bettcha.com. I can check my old address for now, but not for much longer, so—<u>again</u>—please make note of this <u>new</u> <u>e-mail</u> <u>address</u>. Thank you, thank you, thank you!)

Anyway, Paul, your "conference" plans must've fallen through in the end, huh? (Or you were trying to avoid me—and look where <u>that</u> got you! Just kidding . . . :-)) After I realized it was you I'd knocked into, I wanted to buy you a drink (or let you buy me one!) and really talk seriously about what's going on here with our e-mail correspondence, because I think it's pretty special. But I completely understand that with a bashed nose and blood streaming everywhere (and your "friend" yelling at me and acting as though he were trying to "hold you back"—what was <u>that</u> all about?), you needed to get thee to a doctor! But what a lost opportunity. :-(

I do hope you're better now. And I hope you know that I "get it" when it comes to being stretched thin. I <u>completely</u> sympathize with how very, <u>very</u> busy you must be, Paul. You're an "esteemed" author, after all! (If only we were <u>all</u> that busy! Just kidding . . . :-))

So, no pressure (<u>really</u>!), but when you do get two minutes—two <u>seconds</u> even—I've done some more work on my novel and would love your input. I've attached a revision.

Lastly, believe it or not, I ended up writing a draft of the clowns story! The working title is "City Clown, Country Clown." Nice, eh? Your idea was just too tempting; I couldn't resist. But maybe we should collaborate! We could just e-mail revisions back and forth. Actually, if you want, why don't you simply track or note any changes you make to the attached file, then I can accept (or not!) each change when you send the story back to me. Easy enough, yes?

So, until next time, my friend! By the by, I really do love Will o' the Wisp and can see why you'd make it your regular hangout. (I may have to do the same!) Let me know when you want to meet up there again. Obviously, we'll have to be extra vigilant walking through any and all doorways! :-)

Best of the best,
Tim

PS—FYI, Paul, I Googled you again when I realized I don't know where you live. Your alma mater popped up in one of the search results, so I was able to hunt down your address on your college website (which seemed none too secure, I have to say!). Anyway, if I happen to find myself in your "nabe," I'll swing by. Maybe tomorrow afternoon? Let me know if that works for you!

Jimmy Jenkins

JIMMY JENKINS AND CHRISTOPHER EASTMAN
MAKE SOME TROUBLE

1976

Jimmy Jenkins's mother is downstairs watching television. *Masterpiece Theatre* or some other show from England with no laugh track, and nothing funny about it anyway. Exactly the kind of thing your parents would be home watching if they weren't attending the faculty dance at Harrison Cutler Prep, where your father is the dean. And here you are, Jimmy and you, in Jimmy's room with a fresh bag of Nacho Cheese Doritos you stole from the kitchen pantry. His mother heard you rooting around in there after supper and said, "You boys are making a racket. Jimmy, Christopher, go find something constructive to do and let me hear my program."

Jimmy is two years older than you. When you're together, he's usually the one who comes up with the good idea, some way to have fun or make a little trouble, like those times he got you to sneak cigarettes from your father's pack of Pall Malls. The two of you crouched behind the holly bushes outside your house and toked away until you were dizzy. Drag-drunk, Jimmy called it. And there was the night in August when he swiped a couple of Old Milwaukees from his mother's fridge. You and he sped along Blanke Street to that isolated stretch where a jungle of sticker bushes and weed trees presses in on either side. You took turns guzzling from the cans until your belly got all bloated up and the beer was thick and heavy and hard to suck down. Jimmy just laughed at you and finished off both beers himself.

It's January now, and you've just celebrated your thirteenth birthday. At school, you've bragged to your friends about your adventures with Jimmy, but lately there's been nothing to brag about: The Old Mils and the Pall Malls were months ago. Now that you're a teenager, maybe it's your turn to come up with the good idea.

Jimmy lies on his bed, munching chips one after another as though he's forgotten you're even there. Standing in the doorway, you bring your thumb to your lips and tilt your head back like you're chugalugging. "Hey, man, wanna do some drinkin'?"

Jimmy swivels off the bed. He tugs you into the room and closes the door. "My mom's not deaf, you know." He glares at you as he wipes the orange Doritos yuck from the corners of his mouth. "What the hell are you talking about?"

"I thought we could take some beers like we did last summer."

"No way, Junior. Not with my mom right outside the

kitchen. There's nothing in the refrigerator anyway. I checked."

You sit next to each other on the edge of the bed, kicking at the floor, until Jimmy says, "Wait, what about *your* parents? We could break into their liquor cabinet."

Beer is one thing, but liquor? You remember the Fall camporee out at Lake Pamunkey when a kid from your grade snuck off with a few of the older scouts, put away half a pint of Wild Turkey, then staggered back to the campfire and threw up on Scoutmaster Peterson's boots. That awful smell: wet smoke and chili con carne and upchuck.

And there's the new sitter your parents have hired to look after you and your two little sisters—Rose-Ann Shapcott, one of your father's students at Cutler. Your curfew is at ten. Won't Rose-Ann be suspicious if you show up early with Jimmy, then duck out again?

"We just tell her we're getting some albums," Jimmy says.

"I guess," you say, remembering how the drunk kid at the camporee had groaned and dry-heaved outside his tent for hours.

-+-

At your house, Rose-Ann is watching *Donny & Marie* with Penny and Amanda in the basement-level rec room. One flight above, you and Jimmy sneak into the kitchen, literally tiptoeing, but then you hear Rose-Ann calling your name and her shoes click-clacking on the steps. Seconds later, she rounds the corner: long, flyaway auburn hair, pale green eyes, and a small gap between her two front teeth, like that model you've seen on the covers of your mother's magazines. Rose-Ann is curvy too, unlike the seventh-grade girls, who are either plump or knobby-boned and skinny, no curves at all.

You pick up the box of Nutter Butters that's sitting out on the kitchen table. "We're just getting a snack, then we're gonna grab some records and head back out." But she's not even listening; she's all eyes for Jimmy.

"Wow, you look *just like* your brother," she says. "I knew him before I started at Cutler. You're in ninth grade, right?"

Jimmy's ears glow pink. "Yep." He doesn't like being compared to his brother, Matt, a senior this year and one of the starting runningbacks for the Brookford High Bucks.

"Must feel good, last year of junior high."

Jimmy shrugs. "It's okay."

Rose-Ann takes a cookie from the box you're holding and leans back against one of the counters. "So who do you have for Earth Science?"

"Mr. Goodlaw."

"Oh my God, you're so lucky. I had Mr. Neer." She sticks out her tongue. "Mr. Sneer. We used to say, 'How far from Neer?'"

"Not far enough," Jimmy says, with a grin.

Rose-Ann grins too. "I guess everyone knows the same old jokes," she says, before taking a bite of her Nutter Butter.

From the rec room comes the sound of a miniature ava-lanche—wooden blocks falling to the floor, marbles skitter-ing everywhere. Amanda, the younger of your sisters, starts crying.

"Oh shit," says Rose-Ann, "I'll talk to y'all later." She pops the rest of the cookie into her mouth, pinches up her hippie peasant dress on either side, and hurries back down-stairs, the soles of her leather clogs click-clacking on the steps again.

You wait until you hear Rose-Ann talking to your sis-ters—assuring them in soothing tones that everything is going to be all right—before easing open the oak-paneled cabinet door next to the stove. The top two shelves of the cabinet are stocked with green, brown, and clear glass bot-tles. Pints, fifths, half-gallons. One, squat and ample, ap-pears to be filled with melted raspberry sherbet. Another, tall and narrowing, looks like Barbara Eden's bottle on *I Dream of Jeannie.*

"*Damn,*" Jimmy says. "You got a jar or something we can fill up?"

You check the space under the kitchen sink. It's crowded with empty sixteen-ounce Coke bottles, a dozen or so your mother hasn't returned to the A&P yet.

"Take two," he says. "We'll need one for a chaser. Juice or something, unless you've got more Coke somewhere."

You set the bottles on the counter and open the fridge: No soda or real juice of any kind—no OJ or even grapefruit juice, which your father enjoys for some inexplicable rea-son—but there is a large can of the red Hawaiian Punch you and your sisters like to drink at breakfast. "No more Coke. How's this?"

"Guess it'll have to do," Jimmy says. He takes the can and, leaning over the sink, begins pouring the punch into one of the empty bottles. Some dribbles down the side. "Man, we're gonna get caught," he says. He pours a little more, then stops and looks at his reflection in the multi-paned window above the sink. "Rose-Ann's probably cool, though. Wish I'd met her before. She is *sweet.*"

After topping up the bottle, he closes his thumb over the lip and holds it under one flap of his Michelin Man parka. "You fill up the other one and meet me by the bushes." You nod as he strides across the kitchen floor. When he reaches the doorway, he whispers over his shoulder, "Don't fuck up."

In three quick trips up the back stairs, you carry to your bedroom two fifths and a half-gallon bottle of liquor, the empty Coke bottle, the can of Hawaiian Punch, and a plastic funnel, which you were smart enough to think of and found in the back of a utility drawer.

As you arrange everything on the thin area rug next to your bed—carefully, like you're handling volatile compounds in a bomb-making factory—you notice the extra blanket your mother has put out for you, folded in a tidy square on top of your pillow. It's the one you've had since kindergarten with the repeating pattern of red and gold toy soldiers marching in line. Why hasn't she gotten rid of it by now? You remember how, when you were little, she would bring your covers up under your chin and say, "Tuck-in time for Topher the Gopher." She'd give you an Eskimo kiss and sing "Down by the Station." Whenever your parents hosted a late-night dinner party, their guests' chatter and the sounds of glass and silverware all clinking together would echo up from the dining room. Your mother's breath would be smoky and boozy-sweet, an intimate smell you still associate with that early time, when neither of your parents were afraid to nuzzle you.

As you look down at the liquor bottles, the memories start to make you feel a little guilty and uneasy. But then you laugh to yourself, wondering what your mother would think of her little Topher the Gopher now, stealing her booze for himself.

The half-gallon bottle is gin, and one of the fifths is whiskey—Ten High bourbon. On your knees, with the Coke bottle in front of you, the stem of the funnel in its mouth, you pour from one bottle, then the next, watching the liquid slosh and mix together. The second fifth is some fancy-brand vermouth. You're not exactly sure what vermouth is, but it doesn't smell nearly as strong as the gin or the whiskey. That's probably a good thing. You add some to the mixture. Last, the Hawaiian Punch, which you figure will help the liquor go down easier. You pour in a few ounces, until the Coke bottle is full.

After rinsing the funnel in the upstairs bathroom, you return everything to the kitchen, trying to remember the exact positions of the liquor bottles before you took them—and panicking for a moment when you realize you're not quite sure. Then you go back for the Coke bottle in your room. You hold on to it the same way Jimmy held on to his, with your thumb over the lip.

Outside, there's a full moon overhead, casting black, hard-edged shadows onto the green-gray landscape. Brookford hasn't seen any snow yet this winter, and you're thankful that the night air isn't too cold. Jimmy is waiting by the holly bushes. "What the hell took you so long?" he mutters as the two of you hurry along the sidewalk.

✤

Miss Linny Mae Hawkins lives alone in an old Victorian mansion down the street from Jimmy's. Everyone calls it the Castle. Miss Linny Mae is ninety-five and, from what you can tell, never leaves her bedroom. From the sidewalk, you see the flicker of blue television light in an upstairs window. You and Jimmy slink along the flagstones leading around to her backyard, a maze of hedges, small lawns, and terraced garden beds, all enclosed by a high brick wall. You sit on the ground, scrunched next to each other with your backs against the trunk of a big Indian-cigar tree.

"You mixed bourbon, gin, *and* vermouth?" Jimmy says. "*And* that red stuff?"

"I thought it would taste better."

"Kool-Aid doesn't make liquor taste better, Junior." He sniffs at the mouth of your bottle, shudders, and hands it right back to you. "Be my guest."

Your first sip goes down like fruit-flavored gasoline. You gasp for air; your eyes tear up. But Jimmy is there with the chaser, and you guzzle from it until your throat stops burning.

Jimmy's next. He takes two or three short swigs. His eyes water too, but instead of reaching for the chaser right away, he stares off across the yard, gritting his teeth and flaring his nostrils, before finally sipping from the bottle of punch. "*Whew*, that is harsh," he says. He grins at you, though, and you take it as an acknowledgment that he's enjoying himself, that you've done good.

The two of you pass the bottle back and forth, always keeping the punch handy so you don't cough and choke. You sit with your knees pulled into your chest, dreading your next turn. But when your turn does come and you're holding the bottle, Jimmy's on his feet. Riding an imaginary skateboard, arms thrust out and teeter-tottering. Or pretending that he's making out with someone, back turned toward you, fingers massaging his shoulders and the sides of his neck. Or marching in place like a drill-corps marine, calling "Sir, yes sir!" and saluting toward the roof line of the Castle.

You've never seen Jimmy this animated before. Usually he wears a scowl and peeks out from beneath his dirty-blond bangs with narrowed eyes, as if nothing around him is worth his time or attention. You're normally the one acting silly—making fart noises, doing George Carlin impressions, singing Kiss and Queen and Mott the Hoople songs in a cracking falsetto. Jimmy always turns his scowl on you and says, "Be cool!"

Soon the Hawaiian Punch chaser is gone, but an inch of

the liquor mix is left, one final gulp for each of you. Jimmy stands over you with the bottle. "One for the money, shoe for the toe," he says, and tips his head back for a swallow. He hands you the bottle and weaves across the yard, eventually lying on the ground next to a row of bare forsythia bushes.

You bring the bottle under your nose, gagging at the syrupy aroma of this last half-ounce of backwash. You take a deep breath before draining the rest of the liquor. Your stomach clenches for a second, then relaxes.

Jimmy is talking to himself. He toddles back over to the tree. "Cuntler," he says, chuckling. "Was thinking about those foxy Cuntler Prep girls, like . . . what's her name?"

"Rose-Ann?"

"Yes! Ro-*Zay*! She is *fine*," he says, pacing back and forth. "Know what I mean, Junior? Like Lauren Hutton or something. Course, my old man woulda said, 'Women: Can't live with 'em, can't shoot 'em.'"

This is only the second time you've ever heard Jimmy mention his father. The first was when your sister Penny—out of the blue, when you and Jimmy were shooting hoops in your driveway—asked Jimmy what his daddy did.

"He's dead," said Jimmy, watching the ball he'd just shot swish through the net.

All you know is what your parents have told you, that Colonel Jenkins returned home from Vietnam and was killed in a car wreck only a few months later. Jimmy was in the fourth grade. You didn't know him then, but you've wondered whether his heavy-hooded eyes and constant half-frown are because of all the crying he must have done at the time. Can you cry so much that it changes the way you look for the rest of your life?

Jimmy is marching in place and saluting again, his elbow high in the air. "Sir! Major Jenkins and Private Junior Samples reporting for duty, sir!" He nods at you and laughs. "Man, this is cool. I haven't been in this yard since me and my brother used to play army here."

You can't believe how tipsy Jimmy is, especially since you don't feel much of anything yet. The moon wiggles and wobbles a little when you blink up at it, but that's all. You pull your knit toboggan cap down over your ears and stand up.

You fall down. Jimmy laughs. His black Chuck Taylors are half an inch from your face. "On your feet," he says. "We gotta get over to the 7-Eleven and swipe some munchies."

You're on all fours, then you're hugging the trunk of the tree. You're on the other side of the yard and Jimmy is talking about Lauren Hutton again. You remember something.

"Records," you say.

"What?"

"Forgotta bring the *records*. We tole Rose-Ann." You feel like you're talking under water.

You stumble along Miss Linny Mae's front walk, with Jimmy saying, "Get it together, Chris." Then you're half-way up Blanke Street, Jimmy has pulled you into the weed-tree woods, and you can't figure out what you keep tripping over. You're dimly aware that he's back to his usual scowly self. "How can you be this fucking drunk?"

Next, you're at your front door—how did you get here?—and Rose-Ann is asking what you've been drinking. You squeeze by her, slipping on the stairs that lead down to the rec room. You make it to the couch to watch television, but Jimmy is standing in front of you, blocking the screen, saying, "She knows, man. She's not stupid."

Then you're kneeling over the toilet in the downstairs bathroom, puking your guts out for what seems like hours, before finally crawling up the carpeted front stairs toward your bedroom. Between the balusters, you spy Jimmy sitting next to Rose-Ann on the living room sofa. "Is this fun?" you say.

Rose-Ann stands up. Jimmy looks like he wants to sock you. "*What?*" he says.

"I thought this was s'posed to be fun."

❖

Your father taps twice on your bedroom door and pokes his head in. "How's everyone in the ICU?"

"Better." You make no effort to sit up in bed, afraid the room will start spinning again.

"Rose-Ann told us you got sick last night," he says. "There's a stomach flu going around. Your number must've been up." He stands above you in his corduroy suit and speckled tie, smiling his wide, asymmetrical smile. "It's almost ten. We're off to church. You all right here alone, Chris?"

"Yes, sir, I'm just gonna try and sleep some more."

He pats your knee. "Okay then. But call the church office if you need us."

You do feel as if you have the flu—achy, with a cottony mouth and an empty gurgling stomach—so it's not difficult to fake sick, which you do, all day Sunday and for a couple days after that. Your parents don't seem to suspect anything. They must have come home as drunk as you did on Saturday night not to have noticed something out of place or detected a trace of alcohol in the air. But maybe they're just used to trusting you.

On Monday and Tuesday, you stretch out on the rec room couch, watching game shows in the morning, reruns of *Andy Griffith* and *My Favorite Martian* in the afternoon, while your mother brings you ginger ale and honey toast and baked potatoes. Any time she leaves the house on an errand, you sneak a Pop Tart or a bowl of cereal. But then on Wednesday morning, after convincing your parents that you're feeling pretty much back to normal, you return to school—Stonewall Jackson Junior High.

At lunch, you sit with a couple of your friends, treating them to all the details: Jimmy and Rose-Ann and Miss Linny Mae's castle, the liquor and the Hawaiian Punch. They chew in silence as you talk, interrupting only with an occasional *"Man"* or "No shit?"

You notice Jimmy and several of his ninth-grade friends

hanging around the back of the cafeteria in their identical ink-blue parkas, ready to step outside for a smoke before the bell rings. A few of them have started calling Jimmy by a new nickname: Jinx. Probably because it sounds cool. So far, he hasn't let on that you should call him that, but you're sure it's only a matter of time before he does. After emptying your tray, you tell your friends you'll catch up with them later and walk over to Jimmy and his buddies. He barely acknowledges your presence.

"My parents think I had the flu," you say. "I didn't tell them—"

"You *best* not tell them anything, Junior," he says. "Understand?"

Archie Wagner, one of the guys who got the seventh-grader drunk on the Lake Pamunkey camporee, smirks. "Jinx told us you had some trouble holding your liquor, big guy. You and that other kid from scout camp should start a band, call yourselves the Pukes, you know what I'm sayin'?" He, Jimmy, and the rest of the group snicker and file out the door.

Over the next few weeks, you run in to Jimmy at school from time to time, or see him down the hall or across the cafeteria. He jerks his chin in your direction, as he always has. But he stops coming by your house or having you over to his place for supper.

"It was bound to happen," your father says. "He's older now, with different interests. Next year he'll be at the high school."

Still, though, you and your seventh-grade friends continue to comb your hair back in long, feathered layers and sport your faded flannel shirts and straight-leg Levi's, copying the dress code that Jimmy and his crew follow so effortlessly. And at night, you pray to God, asking Him to make you as cool as you can be. As cool as Jimmy.

-:-

On an unseasonably warm Saturday afternoon in March, your father calls you into the living room. He and your mother are sitting in the room's wingback chairs in their church clothes. His usual off-kilter smile is upside down, a stern off-kilter frown that you very rarely see. Your mother is fanning herself with one of her magazines, and her face is red, like she's been crying—or is embarrassed, or furious, about something. Or all three.

"We need to talk to you about the night Rose-Ann Shapcott was here," your father says, motioning over his shoulder with his thumb, as if pointing two months back in time. "That night you got sick."

Your blood begins to race as you stand in front of them. "Yes, sir?"

"Do you remember anything out of the ordinary?" He shakes his head as if the question isn't quite right and tries again. "Was *Rose-Ann* acting unusual?"

Have they noticed that their liquor bottles appear out of place? After all this time? "No," you say, trying to keep your voice steady. "She wasn't acting weird or anything."

Your parents exchange unhappy glances.

"Mom is missing some jewelry," your father says. "The necklace I gave her for Christmas."

Your mother stops fanning herself. "With the garnet stones," she says. "I *know* you've heard us talking about this."

You don't recall her saying anything about it, but she squinches her eyebrows together with such a look of impatience that you say, "Oh, right."

"We've traced everything back," says your father, "and we're fairly sure—"

"We're *positive*," your mother says.

Your father sighs quietly and rubs his forehead. "*Yes . . .* the necklace went missing right around the time Rose-Ann was here. In fact, son, we suspect she took it. We're driving to the Shapcotts now to meet with Rose-Ann and her parents. They're over on Monarch Drive. We're going to have to confront her about all of this."

You let your breath go, surprised by this news, but relieved that your parents haven't found out about you and Jimmy getting drunk.

"We needed to make sure you didn't know anything about this whole mess," your father says. "Of course, what we've told you doesn't leave this room."

Unsettled by your parents' interrogation, you go to the liquor cabinet after they've driven away in the family station wagon. Your sisters are down the street at a friend's, so you have the house to yourself. You pour a shot of Smirnoff vodka into a tall glass of orange juice and take your cocktail with you to the rec room, where you sip it as you watch the tube. Ever since you heard that Smirnoff screwdrivers were the best, you've wanted to try one. It's delicious: You can barely taste the vodka. So much better than your Hawaiian Punch concoction, which causes you to shiver with disgust when you think about it now.

You think about Rose-Ann too, but your memories of that night are murky. It's difficult to form a completely clear picture of her in your mind. She was so pretty and friendly. You can't imagine she's a jewel thief. Maybe she's a kleptomaniac. Wow, a *klepto*.

Then you wonder: What if—once she's cornered, pinned to the wall by her parents and yours—she spills her guts about you and Jimmy? But she wouldn't do that.

After your drink, in your father's study upstairs, you open the polished wooden box on his desk. You slide three cigarettes from his pack of Pall Malls and take them to your room. Holding one between your lips, you deposit the other two in the plastic baggie you keep in the back of your sock drawer. You've collected seven cigarettes over the past few weeks; now you have nine. The next time you have a couple of friends to your house for a sleepover, you'll each have three. Plus, you've got one for yourself now.

Sitting outside on the back-porch steps hidden from the street, you smoke. You get a little drag-drunk after four or five tokes, but you've learned to enjoy the feeling. You figure your father must have enjoyed it too when he started smoking, probably when he was a teenager like you and Jimmy.

Once you've burned the cigarette down to the filter, you

go out to the street and flick the butt into the gutter. You head over to the 7-Eleven on Lee-Jackson Avenue, where you swipe a Baby Ruth bar when the old pink-haired clerk turns her back. Then you kick along the sidewalk, enjoying your candy, taking your time getting home.

After a while, you see the top of Miss Linny Mae's castle above the low, flat-roofed commercial buildings along that stretch of Lee-Jackson. You cut down the side alley of an auto parts store and across a vacant lot to get to Blanke Street. Maybe you can swing by Jimmy's and let him in on what's happening with Rose-Ann. As you pass the houses at the bottom of the street, you imagine him clapping you on the back when you tell him and leading you into his kitchen to grab a snack. Walking past the Castle minutes later—its burnt-red shutters and turrets vivid in the sharp afternoon light—you picture the two of you in Jimmy's room, listening to albums like you used to. Jinx and Junior.

As you continue further up the street, you hear someone shouting. It isn't until you're directly in front of his place, though, that you realize it's Jimmy. He runs from the back of the house to the front yard and starts down the steps to the sidewalk, but stops when he notices you standing there. "I am *not* talking to your parents." He looks up and down the street, seeming to deflate slightly when he sees that you're alone.

"Jimmy, this is *serious*," calls Mrs. Jenkins, now coming to the front yard as well. She's wearing a flowery pink-and-green housedress and white slippers and doesn't move be-

yond the top of the steps when she reaches them, as if un-
willing to cross some imaginary line.

"I told you, we were *drunk*," Jimmy says, without even
glancing back at her.

You don't know what's happening, but it can't be good
if Jimmy is telling his mother about his drinking. Your legs
go weak.

"Christopher, where *are* your parents?" Mrs. Jenkins
says.

"With one of my dad's students."

"The Shapcott girl, *yes*," she says, impatient and cross.
"They called from her house to say they were coming right
over. We thought you were with them."

You stare at her for a few moments, piecing everything
together, before turning back to Jimmy. "*You* took it."

"That stupid necklace," he says. "And now that bitch has
fucking *narc'd* on me."

"Jimmy!" his mother says.

He pushes you out of the way and runs up the sidewalk.
Without thinking, you start after him, but then you hear
quick footsteps behind you, rapid slaps of rubber on the
concrete. Matt Jenkins, Jimmy's big brother, sprints past. He
catches up with Jimmy and puts him in a head lock. "You
little *punk*," he says, spinning him in a circle.

Jimmy whips his elbows, trying to twist himself loose,
but Matt tightens his hold. He swings Jimmy left and right,
then in one move yanks him off his feet and drops him to his
knees. Jimmy claws and punches at his brother's face, which

only makes Matt angrier. He grabs Jimmy by the hair and forces his cheek to the concrete. He holds him down, pressing with both hands, his muscular arms straight and stiff, his knees pinning Jimmy's legs in place.

Watching them, you imagine jumping on Matt, hitting and kicking him to make him stop. You've seen the two argue before, but never anything like this.

Jimmy jerks back and forth beneath his brother, but finally gives up fighting and lies still. "Okay-okay, let me up, god-*dammit*," he whines.

"Boys, that's *enough*," Mrs. Jenkins says.

You can't believe how small and pitiful she sounds. Powerless and insignificant. You turn to see her still standing at the top of her steps—and your parents pulling up in front of the house. They park the car and open their doors to get out.

Matt struts by, gripping Jimmy's upper arm. "He's right here, Mr. Eastman," he says. But your father and mother just glare at you, waiting for an explanation.

⁍

Mrs. Jenkins apologizes to your parents and returns the necklace to your mother. Jimmy had been hiding it in a manila envelope under his mattress. Your father assures her that there's no need for him to call the police.

Jimmy apologizes too when Matt nudges him. "I was gonna give it back," he mumbles. His chin is scratched up and one side of his face is red with scrape marks. He won't look at you when you try to catch his eye. You want to tell him something, but you're not sure what. Maybe assure him that everything will be all right or that the two of you are in this together. But that's not true anymore. He turns away as your father tells you to get in the car.

On the short drive home, you slouch in the backseat of the station wagon. Your parents ride up front in silence. Once you get to the house, they order you into the living room again.

"To say we're disappointed in you," your father begins, as if nothing else needs to be said. But he continues as you gaze at his shoes. "You may have had nothing to do with the necklace, but to go into our liquor cabinet and lie to us—"

"I didn't lie," you say.

"Telling us you had the *flu*?" your mother says, her voice shaking. "Keeping me at your beck and call while you lounged on the damn couch?"

"You're grounded for a month," your father says, "but it's going to be a hell of a lot longer than that before we trust you again."

In your room, you lie on your bed, worrying a little about what your parents said, but thinking mostly about Jimmy. How he'd flopped around on the sidewalk, like a fish too small to keep but thrown on the river rocks rather than tossed back into the stream.

After mulling things over for half an hour, you take the cigarettes from your dresser drawer, unseal the plastic bag, and breathe in the sweet fragrance of the tobacco, before pocketing it and sneaking it into the bathroom. You stand over the toilet for a few minutes, ready to crush the cigarettes and flush them. Instead, you find yourself heading down the hall to your father's study. He's sitting in his armchair, reading. He barely glances at you in the doorway.

"I took something else," you say.

With a sigh, he closes his book in his lap.

You hold up the baggie, and he leans forward, squinting, until he realizes what he's looking at. "For heaven's *sake*, Christopher, I don't know what to do with you."

"Yes, sir," you whisper, waiting for a lecture. But he doesn't say another word, so you walk across the room and put the bag of stolen cigarettes on the edge of his desk.

The Fourth

WILSON HOPEWELL WIELDS THE POPEYE BAT

2003

Saturday afternoon of the holiday weekend, clear and gorgeous, and Wilson Hopewell had plopped himself in a plastic deck chair in front of the garage. He slow-sipped from a longneck bottle of Budweiser while Adam, his three-year-old, zoomed up and down the driveway on his Road Racer tricycle, his chubby little legs pumping hard and fast.

"Frickin' finally," Wilson said to himself, "a little R and R." With his free hand, he adjusted his cargo shorts, which were bunching between his legs, and smoothed the front of his shirt—the hibiscus-paneled Hawaiian shirt he'd treated himself to at the beginning of the summer—before sinking lower in the chair.

It was then that he noticed the bees again. Three of them. Flitting near the gutters of the garage and droning in circles above its aluminum roof. The same ones he'd wanted to kill that morning when he'd first seen them. Would've killed too, but he'd been in a hurry to get to the annual parade through Brookford's downtown. Anxious to score a decent parking spot, he'd sped off with the boys—Adam and his big brother, Jeremy—and promptly forgotten all about the bees. Now here they were again. Of course. Where would they have gone?

"Son of a *bitch*." He set his half-drunk beer on the pavement and pushed himself out of the chair, only then wondering whether Adam had heard him cussing. His wife, Valerie, had already cautioned him, not twenty-four hours previously, to watch his language around the kids. But the boy was out of earshot, negotiating the turn at the end of the driveway, so Wilson headed into the garage, keeping a close eye on the bees as he snuck under them.

Hanging from nails, screws, and hooks on the garage walls, and poking out of empty paint cans and cardboard boxes along the floor's perimeter, were all of his work tools and lawn implements. He studied one after the other but couldn't decide which was right for the job. Straight-claw hammer? No. Tine-welded bow rake? No. Snow shovel? Garden spade? Foldable trench digger? No, no, *no*.

Then he spied the rope-handled tub the boys kept their outdoor toys in, balanced atop the leaning tower of snow tires in one of the back corners. A plastic baseball bat was sticking out of the tub, and Wilson grabbed it. The hollow red bat was custom-made for little kids, with a narrow handle but a broad barrel four times the size of a regular bat. The Popeye Bat, Wilson liked to call it, its cartoonish shape reminding him of how Popeye's forearms ballooned out below his skinny biceps. Wilson flipped it into the air and caught it with his other hand. He swished it back and forth in front of him like a sword, making light-saber sound effects by humming and whistling at the same time—a pre-*Star Wars* trick he'd learned as a member of the Four Fuckers, the suburban-neighborhood "gang" he'd started with three of his friends back in late elementary school. Then he strutted out of the garage and turned to size up the enemy.

Carpenter bees, that's what they were. Fat and fuzzy. Like bumblebees on steroids. Except they weren't pollinators, Wilson was fairly certain. Could they even sting? It didn't matter: He didn't want them around, scaring the boys and drilling into the garage rafters. He'd swat them onto the pavement and squish them with his heel. The Popeye Bat was super light—easy to swing—and wouldn't damage the siding or gutters of the garage if it thwacked against them. Plus, the barrel's nice big sweet spot would make connecting with each bee a cinch.

"Daddy, look!" Adam called from behind him.

Wilson heard the boy pedaling down the driveway again. "Yeah, buddy, good for you," he called back.

"Look!" cried Adam. "Look, Daddy!"

Wilson finally did turn to look, just in time to see Adam— who was glancing over his shoulder—swerve sharply to the right and plow into the short brick wall that bordered the driveway. He bounced off the trike's handlebars, tumbled onto the pavement, and sat up wailing, tears and snot streaming down his face.

Wilson dropped the bat and jogged over. "You okay, little man?" he said, scooping up his son. "I told you to be careful. You weren't watching, were you?"

Adam's screaming only pitched higher, like an ambulance siren hardwired to Wilson's brain. "Not in my ear, son, not in Daddy's *ear*," Wilson said, getting the boy's attention at last, his heaving sobs downshifting to a steady whine before petering out into sputtering coughs and sniffles.

Wilson reached for the handkerchief in his side pocket. "All right now, you're fine. Let's just blow your nose real good." But Adam didn't wait for the hankie. He blew full-force through his nostrils onto Wilson's shirt and wiped his nose along one of the sleeves. "Son!" Wilson said. He held Adam away from him at arm's length, a thin cable of mucus connecting his shoulder to Adam's upper lip, but pulled the boy close once more when he started crying again. "Oh, it's all right, Adam," he said. "It's only Daddy's favorite shirt." He sighed, thinking how much he'd looked forward to the weekend.

⁘

The day before, Wilson's boss at the insurance company in Turnersburg where he worked had flicked the office lights off and on at three o'clock and told everyone to get the hell out before he changed his mind. On the drive home, thirty minutes along the interstate and another ten across town, Wilson had rolled down the windows of his old Ford Fiesta. Although he'd always loved that name and still liked to think of it as his party machine, it was now speckled with rust and the air conditioner had long ago stopped putting out anything other than hot, oily-engine stink. The radio, though, continued to work fine. Wilson cranked the volume and drummed his fingers on the steering wheel, jamming along with everything the Classic 96.3 station played: "Fly Like an Eagle," "Freebird," "Born to Be Wild." The wind whipped through the car as blasts of bass-guitar distortion thumped him in the chest, making him feel giddy.

Once he'd exited the interstate and driven most of the way to his neighborhood, "Take the Long Way Home" came on. Following the song's advice, Wilson detoured along Blanke Street where Jim "Jenks" Jenkins, a drinking buddy of his, lived. Apparently just home from work himself, still wearing suit pants and a shiny dress shirt he'd untucked, Jenks stood next to the spiraling dogwood tree in his front yard watering the lawn. The spray nozzle in his hand was pointing practically straight up, and a healthy cascade of water rained down in front of him. In his other hand was a tallboy can of Coors. An unlit cigarette was stuck behind his ear.

Wilson turned down the music and pulled over. "Startin' early?" he called.

"Got *that* right," Jenks called back. He grinned and took a pull from his beer.

"There ya *go*," Wilson said. He and Valerie had felt terrible when Jenks's mother had died the previous December, unexpectedly on the day after Christmas. But he was glad to notice lately that his friend now seemed happy to be raising his kids with his wife, Rose-Ann, in the house he'd grown up in. "So where y'all sittin' tonight?"

"Right up front," Jenks said. "Only place to be." He spat on the grass and aimed the hose after it. "Only way to experience fireworks, man."

"Sounds like a plan."

Wilson knew Valerie would hate it there—*right up front.* She'd complain about the crick in her neck from having to gaze directly overhead. She'd grumble that sitting in an aluminum-tube chair made her sciatica pain flare. Meanwhile, the concussive booming of the fireworks would frighten Adam, and Jeremy would endlessly pester his parents for Coke and cotton candy and blue raspberry sno-cones. But Wilson wanted to be where his buddies were. The Fourth came around only once a year. He deserved to enjoy it.

"By the way," Jenks said as he sauntered to another spot in the yard, "how's that re-model of y'all's coming along?"

"Oh my God, don't ask," Wilson said.

Snickering, Jenks shot an arc of water at a mini-copse of azaleas. "Well, I'm sure Valerie's on top of everything."

"Oh yeah, she's got it *all* figured out."

Jenks stopped spraying the hose and gave Wilson a long shrug, as if to say, "Been there, man. What can you do?"

Wilson was tempted to bend Jenks's ear with his latest concerns over Valerie's pet project, the house "improvements" she was coordinating and that he'd originally agreed to—to his ongoing regret. But Jenks had heard most of Wilson's complaints before. Instead, Wilson told Jenks he'd better get on home. "Might as well go find out what today's damage is gonna cost me," he said. "We'll look for you along the fence tonight."

Jenks raised his beer in acknowledgment as Wilson drove away.

Wilson sang along to "Ramblin' Man" before making the final turn onto his own street. In front of his house, a white work van with ladders attached to the top was hiked up on the curb. A silver sports car was parked in the driveway. "Oh boy, the *team*," Wilson said, doing his best varsity-cheerleader imitation. "Rah-frickin'-rah."

He pulled up behind the van, about to head inside when he noticed, all down the block, star-and-stripes bunting draped over porch railings and American flags hanging above front stoops. He wasn't sure whether the display of red, white, and blue simply hadn't caught his eye over the past few days or the neighbors had decided—that morning, apparently—to show off their patriotism all at the same time. Either way, Wilson was glad to see it, and glad that he and the boys had already planted a dozen miniature flags on either side of their own front walk. He sat in the car another minute, taking it all in, listening to the radio until the song ended, before cutting the engine and getting out.

In the living room, where the walls had been stripped and prepped for painting, Valerie was holding a black clipboard in the crook of her arm. Her raccoon sunglasses were balanced on the tip of her nose, and she peered over the lenses at the men gathered in front of her: Gerald the architect, Hugh the designer, and Niko the contractor. (Or was it Miko? Wilson never could remember.) Her team, as she loved to call them.

"Must, Gerry, *must*," Valerie said, as though scolding a

puppy who'd just crapped on a stretch of brand-new carpeting. She emphasized each word with a staccato click of her long nails against the clipboard.

Behind her was the opening into the addition they were building. Although they had a perfectly good family room already, Valerie was certain that this open-plan, multi-purpose space would add prestige and value to the house. Her best friend, Gwen, who lived with her husband and little boy on a beautiful piece of land west of town, had had a similar addition built onto their house the previous fall. Through the thick plastic sheeting that covered the opening, Wilson could make out a table saw and a few five-gallon buckets, but everything was blurry, as if not quite real yet. As if there was still time to make the decision—if they wanted to—to return everything to the way it was before.

"Valerie, we want to make this work," Gerald said, "but with the holiday and all—" He stopped when he noticed Wilson standing inside the front doorway. "Oh, Wilson, hello."

Wilson nodded. "Hey, y'all."

Hugh the designer and Niko/Miko smiled and nodded back. Valerie slid the sunglasses up her nose. "Oh good, you're home," she said. "I'm going to need your help tonight, honey." She walked over and pecked his cheek.

"Looks like everyone got their act together at last," Wilson said, pointing behind him with his thumb.

Valerie stared at him blankly.

"The flags," he said. "The neighbors all have their flags and bunting out. Finally."

"You know, I've been really busy today," she said. "And listen, I need you to feed the kids supper tonight."

"I thought we'd grab something on the way to the fireworks," Wilson said.

Valerie stiffened, jutting her jaw and flaring her nostrils slightly, the face she made when she was either angry or having an orgasm.

"I'm doing my very best to organize our *life* here, Wil," she said. "The fireworks and the flags are not at the top of my priority list at the moment."

"It's the Fourth of July weekend," he said. "Time to take a break."

"No, we're not taking a break. We're working overtime to finish this project."

Wilson felt the back of his neck prickle with heat. "I'm not paying for overtime work."

Valerie tilted her head toward the team enjoying the show: Gerald with a shameless grin on his face; Hugh the designer and Niko/Miko trying not to laugh, examining their own feet as if they'd never seen shoes before. "Can we not talk about this now?" she said.

This was the same discussion they'd been having since March. Wilson actually liked working on the house, enjoyed running errands to Lowe's on the weekends and doing small home repairs. But Valerie's need to keep up with the Joneses had become an obsession—an expensive, seemingly out-of-control obsession that Wilson worried he'd never see the end of. He would have told her this now, as he had numerous times before, except he didn't like the team hovering and listening in any more than she did.

"Fine with me. We don't ever have to talk about it again," he said, immediately regretting how he'd allowed himself to get worked up. Valerie started to say something, but he held up his hands. "Look, you and the guys do your thing. I'll take care of the kids, don't worry." He glanced into the kitchen. "So where *are* they?"

Valerie raised an eyebrow, obviously surprised that he'd kept their argument from escalating. "Adam's up in our room watching a video. Jeremy's outside." She smiled brightly. "He wanted to help water your garden."

"The *tomatoes*?" Wilson said, turning toward the door. "Why would you let him do that?"

Behind the garage, eight-year-old Jeremy was on his knees, attempting to refill a Super Soaker water cannon with the garden hose, which was running full blast. His orange-and-black Orioles cap was flipped around backward and he had his tongue pinched between his teeth. His clothes were so wet that it appeared to Wilson, when he came around the corner, as though his son had fallen off the dock at Lake Pamunkey, where he'd been attending summer day camp with his friends.

"What do you think you're doing?" Wilson said.

"Mom *said* I could," answered Jeremy without looking up.

"She didn't say you could kill them!"

Wilson stared down at his small patch of grape- and cherry-tomato plants tucked against the garage's back wall.

There were fifteen plants total, each a couple of feet high. Most now stood shriveled and dripping, all but drowned by Jeremy's target practice. Several were flattened against the ground. The plot itself, completely flooded, looked like an overflowing sewer: Clumps of soil and dozens of tiny orange and green tomatoes floated like little turds in the brown water.

Wilson grabbed the gun away from Jeremy and tossed it over the high, white-vinyl fence at the edge of the yard, into the gravel alley where they kept their trash barrels. It landed with a clatter.

"Hey!" Jeremy said, jumping to his feet and letting go of the hose, which sprayed water across the front of Wilson's khakis before flopping over into the grass.

"Out of here *now*, before I whoop your butt," Wilson said.

Jeremy snickered. "Whoop your butt, whoop your butt!" He wiggled his bony rear end, then ran across the yard and through the back door. "Mom," Wilson heard him call as soon as he stepped inside, "Dad threw my new water gun away!"

Wilson went around to the front of the garage and turned off the spigot. Lying to the side of the driveway, tipped over next to the blue recycling bin, was the big Boston fern that he and the boys had given Valerie for Mother's Day. Its spider-leg stems, with their brittle-looking fronds, were fanned out on the pavement. The plant's root ball and most of the soil from its clay pot had spilled out on top of them. "Well . . . *shit*," he said.

"Watch your mouth," Valerie said. "The boys will hear you."

He looked up to see her standing on the other side of the screen door that opened onto the back deck. Wilson could hear the team behind her in the den, chuckling. He imagined cranking the water back on and spraying them all with it until they were as soaked as Jeremy, who Valerie had most likely sent upstairs to change.

"What's with the plant we gave you?" Wilson said.

"Oh, honey, I meant to tell you," she said. "Unfortunately, a large fern like that is not going to be the right look for the new space."

Wilson tugged on the hose and began looping it onto its green-metal holder beside the spigot. "Nice," he said. He glanced up again, but Valerie had gone back into the den. Gerald the architect now stood behind the screen. He winked at Wilson before turning away to join the others.

"Maybe hanging in a pizzeria," Wilson heard Valerie say, clueless to the fact that even when she lowered her voice, it still carried for blocks. The team laughed again.

"So until then it's an okay look to have a big dead plant dumped out all over the driveway?" called Wilson, the garden hose limp in his hand.

‡

After Friday's frustrations with Valerie and her team, and then skipping the fireworks after all—in part, an attempt to punish Jeremy for what he'd done to the garden—Wilson had hoped at least to enjoy his Saturday. But the kids had complained and misbehaved during the parade in the morning, and the bees and Adam had now ruined his peace and relaxation in the afternoon. He was still holding the boy, but his son was struggling to be released, kneeing him in the ribs and twisting violently. "Wanna ride bike," he whined.

"Okay, *okay*," Wilson said, and set Adam down. The boy backed the tricycle away from the brick wall, slid onto the metal seat, and zoomed down the driveway again. Wilson marched back over to the Popeye Bat and picked it up.

Two of the bees were zipping back and forth a couple of feet above the garage roof, so Wilson focused on the third one, which had locked itself into an elliptical holding pattern right below one of the gutters. "Oh yeah, you are *mine*," he said. He watched it for a moment, tracking its path, making sure he could anticipate its every move, then swung. The bat bounced off the gutter. The bee dodged it easily. In fact, it barely seemed to notice Wilson or the bat at all.

Wilson drew in a breath and fought to regain his focus. He waited . . . waited . . . swung again. Missed again. This time the bee did take notice and flew right at him. Wilson dipped his head out of the way and whacked it. Halfway through its fall toward the back deck, though, it recovered, buzzing in a tight circle before hurtling toward the peak of the roof.

"Dammit!" Wilson shouted. He jumped as high as he could, chopping at the other two and stirring them into a frenzy. The third bee joined them, and all three zigzagged erratically before taking turns dive-bombing Wilson.

Wilson thrashed wildly with the bat, whipping it through the air with such force that it whistled like a small jet flying directly overhead. He failed to connect with any of the bees but did manage to dent the aluminum framing on the left side of the garage door and slam one of the gutters so hard that it cracked along its seam. The bees didn't connect with him either, but they were quick as they darted at him, much quicker than he'd expected. After bobbing and weaving to avoid them, ducking and sidestepping and whaling away for what felt like fifteen minutes—but couldn't have been more than three—Wilson was completely worn out. In near defeat, he retreated to the side of the garage, wondering how he'd ever gotten so out of shape.

Sucking air, drenched in sweat, he took a quick look and saw that the bees were now circling out over the driveway, confused by his sudden disappearance. He leaned back against the wall, trying to cool himself down in the shade. "Don't know where I went, do you, you stupid bugs?" he whispered.

Just as he started to feel better, he heard one of the bees buzzing close by, an electric-alarm-clock droning right around the corner from where he stood. With renewed vigor, he lifted the bat above his head and stepped onto the driveway again. Adam had rolled up on his tricycle, and instead of hitting the bee, Wilson struck one of the trike's handlebars, narrowly missing the boy's face. The *whang* of the bat against the metal bar, together with Wilson's caveman grunt as he came down hard with Popeye, scared Adam even more than his earlier spill onto the pavement, and he began wailing again, high-pitched hysterics that Wilson knew would have the neighbors peeking out of their windows any second.

Wilson let go of the bat and knelt beside his son, who was kicking his legs and screaming. "It's okay, Adam, it's okay." He patted the boy's back, but Adam only kicked harder and screamed louder.

Valerie had left earlier with Jeremy to stop by the Happy Birthday USA! party that the Brookford Y was hosting. To her keen disappointment, the team had been unavailable to work or even conference-call that day. Wilson looked over now to see her pulling into the driveway.

"What happened?" she said as she stepped out of the car.

Jeremy's usual wise-ass grin vanished as soon as he slid down from the backseat and saw Adam howling.

"Nothing," Wilson said. "He's okay."

Adam cried out even more insistently until Valerie reached him. Whimpering, he climbed into her arms.

"He just got scared. He, uh, fell off his trike," Wilson said, wondering whether God would hurl a lightning bolt out of the sky and sizzle him on the spot. "I was taking care of the bees." He glanced around, but they'd all flown away.

Valerie rubbed Adam's arm and let him sniffle against her shoulder. "Taking *care* of them?"

Wilson nodded toward the bat.

"With *that*?" she said. "Oh, good plan, honey. You're really on top of it all."

Wilson didn't argue or try to explain. He could feel a headache coming on, the beginning of a slight throbbing in his temples, and the cure was another cold Bud. Without looking, he reached for the seat of Adam's tricycle for leverage as he stood up. A fourth bee, a small honeybee that had landed on the seat, stung him square in the middle of his palm.

Wilson leapt two feet off the ground. "Ow!" he shouted, waving his hand in the air. He kicked the tricycle, sending it skidding across the asphalt. Then, like some enormous exotic bird trying to take flight, he began hopping on one foot as he continued to flap his hand. "Frickin' hell!"

The boys were both giggling now.

"Daddy funny," said Adam.

"*Frickin'* funny," said Jeremy.

"Wilson, calm down, please," Valerie said. "Are you all right?"

With his eyes squeezed shut, though, Wilson was only vaguely aware that she was speaking. In spite of the pain he felt, his jumping up and down had a soothing rhythm to it that was beginning to put everything out of his mind. Valerie was saying, "Are you listening to me?" But her voice, like his own breathing, seemed miles away. Only when he almost tripped after a few moments did he finally stand still.

His entire hand was achy and swollen, and the spot on his palm where he'd been stung felt hot and itchy. His big toe pounded. He was certain he'd split it open. He looked over at everyone. At Valerie scowling at him. At Adam squirming in her arms. At Jeremy flitting around Adam's trike. Wilson had an urge to pick up the bat and bounce it off the tops of their heads. But an image popped into his mind. He pictured himself sitting in the middle of the driveway while his family steered around him on Road Racer tricycles, all three of them waving big red Popeye Bats and knocking the hell out of *him*.

The thought made Wilson laugh. Softly at first, almost to himself, but then more loudly, convulsively. Tears began to fill his eyes. When he tried to stop, he inhaled too quickly and his laughter turned into an extended coughing fit.

"What is going on?" Valerie said. "Do you need some water?"

Wilson shook his head and bent forward. With his hands on his knees, he hacked his lungs out while Valerie stood in front of him. He heard the boys run into the backyard, heard Jeremy chasing his little brother, threatening to tickle him, and Adam giggling like crazy. Wilson listened to them until, finally, his coughing began to wane and his breathing evened out.

"Seriously," Valerie said. "Are you okay?"

"I'm fine," Wilson said. "It's just—"

"What."

"Well . . ." He cleared his throat and laughed softly again. "Oh, I don't know. I mean, guys talk this talk about how their family comes first. No one ever flips it around and says, 'Yay, me: I come frickin' dead last.' No one ever *would*. But it's kind of the same thing, you know?" When Valerie didn't answer, he looked up. "I just thought it was funny."

"Give me a break, Wilson," Valerie said. "Listen, I'm sorry you hurt yourself—I really am—but the boys and I aren't here to make your life miserable."

"No, that's not what I *meant*," he said, but she'd already turned away. "Come on, guys," she called to the boys. "Let's go inside and leave Daddy alone. He's having a pity party."

Jeremy sprinted across the yard and up the steps of the deck. "A *frickin'* pity party," he said, and went into the house. Adam toddled over to Valerie and stuck out his bottom lip. "I wanna go to pity potty too!"

"I know you do, honey," Valerie said, "but let's get you a snack first, okay?"

Adam's face lit up. "Juice box?"

Valerie smiled. "Juice box," she said, and picked him up.

Wilson tried again. "Val, I'm not having a pity party. I'm just trying to explain—"

"We'll talk about it later," she said over her shoulder as she walked up the steps carrying Adam. "Or"—she stopped on the deck and turned to face Wilson—"fine with me if we never talk about it again." Then she went inside, the screen door slapping shut behind her.

Wilson watched the door for a moment before wiping his eyes, flinching against the pain in his hand. The bee that had stung him lay on the ground near Adam's trike, and he limped over, ready to crush it if it showed any signs of life. It didn't, but he squashed it anyway. He started to head inside too, but then thought better of it. Instead, he plopped himself down in his chair again. The summer sun was still high in the sky, and he tilted his head back to feel the heat full on his face. He imagined that the sudden quiet all around him, the first quiet he'd had all weekend, was something to celebrate.

Route

BILLY PATTERSON, CURT RALSTON, AND
ADVENTURES IN NEWSPAPER DELIVERY

1979

Billy Patterson moseyed up Lee-Jackson Avenue, canvas delivery sack over one shoulder, front pockets bulging with a hundred pink rubber bands. He still had on his school clothes—Levi's cords and the plaid button-down his grand-parents had sent him for his birthday in July—but before leaving the house he'd untucked the shirt and changed into a favorite old pair of Chuck Taylor hi-tops.

As he climbed the long hill, he kicked a piece of gravel ahead of him, then a bottle cap, then a flattened beer can, which skidded over the sidewalk with a nice metallic rattle. Occasionally, he glanced to his right to take in the view: Brookford's downtown, its stocky brick buildings and the clock tower on Third Street; and beyond, the patches of farmland that disappeared into a blue haze where they met the mountains on the horizon. It was a warm afternoon in late September and Billy was happy to take his time, certain that his newspapers wouldn't be waiting for him anyway. Archie Wagner and Jinx Jenkins, the high-school potheads who dropped them off, were always late.

Sure enough, when he reached the corner of Monarch Drive at the top of the hill, all he saw on the side of the road were some stray loops of twine from deliveries earlier in the week. Along the sidewalk was a low stone wall, and Billy hopped up onto it and sat, bouncing the heels of his sneakers against the wall and watching the cars cruise along Lee-Jackson.

Short and skinny, small for thirteen, Billy wasn't surprised that no one noticed him there. Most of the drivers gazed ahead expressionless or sang along with their music, unaware they were being observed. A few appeared to be having heated conversations with themselves. One guy in a brand-new Datsun—a silver-haired man Billy recognized from church—had a finger up his nose. Billy laughed and shot a rubber band at the car's taillights.

Ten minutes later, the *Brookford Guardian* delivery van came cruising along the avenue as well. It pulled over, its side door already sliding open as it rocked to a stop, and Archie chucked a stack of papers onto the sidewalk. An older guy wearing mirrored sunglasses who Billy had never seen before sat behind the steering wheel chewing on a toothpick.

Billy got down from the wall and poked his head inside the back of the van, the windowless space reeking of motor oil, body odor, and pot smoke. "Hey Archie, where's Jinx?" he said.

Surrounded by scores of newspaper bundles, Archie

wound his long hair behind one ear. "That fuckin' a-hole didn't show up today. Can you believe that shit, man?" He smiled. "And listen, big guy, I told you to call me Wags, all right?" He closed the door as Billy nodded, and the van took off into Lee-Jackson traffic, directly in front of a gold Camaro, which braked with a squeal, horn blasting. Billy watched until the car sped up again before pulling the loops of twine off his stack.

On the front page of today's edition was a shot of Mount Warren that appeared to have been taken near Billy's house. The black-and-white photo made the small mountain look like a flat, inky mass with a few puffy clouds above it, like something a first-grader would create using finger-paint and cotton balls. Billy skimmed the photo's caption: Brookford officials were concerned about teenage "revelers" leaving beer cans and other trash along the gravel access road to the scenic picnic area at the top of Mount Warren. People in town were asking whether the road should be closed after dark.

As he thumbed through his papers, Billy decided that he didn't have a problem with older kids getting together on the mountain at night. He liked the idea of them running free through the woods, away from home and school for a while. There wasn't much else for them to do in Brookford anyway, and the juniors and seniors he knew—like Jinx and Wags (he smiled at the mobster-sounding nicknames)—were okay. Billy had tried beer a time or two but wasn't sure yet whether he wanted to smoke pot and get drunk for real when he got a little older. It seemed like fun.

For now, he needed to concentrate on his papers. After counting out forty-seven and putting those into his bag, he set the remaining twenty-two on the wall, holding them down with a brick he kept there for that purpose. His route took him to the end of Monarch Drive and then back along Altamont Road, one block over, returning him to Lee-Jackson and the drop-off point again. He'd pick up the second stack for the final stretch, down the big hill toward his house.

Wednesday's papers were the heaviest of the week, not counting Sunday, and Billy strained under the weight of the bag as he took a left down Monarch. They were hard to roll up too. But Billy knew how to handle them, folding each one over twice and shimmying a rubber band around it. By the time he got to his first house, he had a dozen ready to go.

He lobbed one between two magnolia trees onto Mrs. Tinsley's porch. It slid and thumped against her storm door. Across the street, he underhanded the next one at the foot of the Shapcotts' long driveway, disappointed that the good-looking daughter, Rose-Ann, had returned to college after a summer of sunbathing in the front yard in her bikini. The two houses after that, one-story cottages with wide stoops in front, were easy shots. One, two, Billy aimed and scored.

Most of the houses on Monarch Drive were white colonials, with neat lawns, boxwood-lined walkways, and rhododendron bushes under bay windows. Billy imagined he was throwing a football or taking a basketball hook shot every time he tossed a paper onto a front porch or step. He even made a game out of the special-request houses. He was a burglar when he tiptoed up the back stairs of the lady who worked nights at the hospital and had asked Billy to quietly leave her paper under her mat. Three houses later, he was a hit man on the prowl for Colonel Reese, who liked his paper laid out flat next to the wicker chair on his screened-in porch. It was a thrill for Billy going to these places he wouldn't have known about otherwise: down flagstone paths, into backyard rose gardens, through private side entrances. He was always sorry when he came to the end of Monarch, and today was no exception. After delivering to the last house, he stood looking back at the long curve of the street, enjoying how the afternoon sun lit up the houses on the east side and, behind them, the wall of towering white pines that divided the neighborhood from Altamont Road. Above the forest, in the distance, stood Mount Warren, its impressive, leaf-green bulk beginning to show patches of rust and gold that the newspaper photo simply couldn't reproduce.

Knowing he had to keep going, though, Billy soon turned and hiked along the dirt trail that led to the bottom of Altamont, his least favorite part of the route. Although several of the houses on the street had been fixed up, most were run down, with busted windows and crumbling front walks and rail-less sagging porches. And Billy never knew, from one week to the next, exactly who he was delivering to. A few of the houses on Altamont had been divided into rental apartments whose tenants came and went, sometimes without settling their bills. The ones he was able to collect from always met him with suspicious eyes, never inviting him in but instead closing their front doors in his face and stranding him there while they searched for loose change.

"Those are hardworking people," his mother had said when he'd told her how unfriendly they were. "You're to be on your best behavior out there, you hear me?"

But she wasn't the one getting heckled by the shirtless drunk man and his buddies when the van brought the papers two hours late. Or yelled at by the mean-looking woman with the thick, sky-blue eyeshadow who claimed she was all paid up when he tried to collect: "You callin' me a liar, boy?" He'd never had adults speak to him with so much hatred in their voices.

Speeding along now, his delivery sack half empty, Billy threw papers to the first of the houses on Altamont. The street seemed quiet today: No engines revving or large dogs barking behind chain-link fences, and no one outside as far as he could see. He began to hope that he could finish this part of the route without running into anyone.

Then he passed in front of Curt Ralston's house, a brick ranch that sat back from the sidewalk beneath a giant maple. Billy glanced over and there was Curt, staring at him above the cinder-block half wall attached to one end of the house. "Hey, Patterson," he said, "come here a minute." His laugh sounded like a wet cough. Billy heard someone behind Curt laughing too.

"Gotta finish my route," Billy said.

Curt leaned out over the wall, his floppy red hair falling across his face. "I don't give a fuck. I said get your ass over here *now*. I wanna show you something."

Curt was fifteen, but he'd been held back twice in school and was still only in the eighth grade, same as Billy. He'd picked on Billy when they were younger, but these days, especially since they didn't share any classes at the junior high, Billy was able to steer clear of him. He managed to avoid him even when he delivered the papers. This was the first time he'd run into Curt since starting the route back in May.

Pressing his lips together, Billy walked up the Ralstons' gravel driveway and around the half wall to a cement patio hidden from the street.

Curt was perched on a metal stool with his heels on a rung just below the seat. Next to him, Randy Hayes, a beefy kid from the neighborhood, sat cross-legged on the cement floor. Both wore jeans and black T-shirts, Randy's advertising a brand of tequila Billy had never heard of. There was a Styrofoam cooler full of beer between them, and empty bottles and cans were lined up on a picnic-table bench set to one side.

Curt reached behind him and brought up a clear glass bottle of Miller High Life. An inch of white foam floated at the top. "Look what I got for you," he said to Billy. His eyes were bloodshot, and he struggled to keep from laughing. Randy just grinned and stared at Curt.

"No thanks, man, that's okay," Billy said.

Curt held the bottle out toward him. "C'mon now, Patterson, drink up."

Thinking this probably wasn't the best idea, but unsure of what Curt and Randy might do if he refused, Billy took the bottle. After all, he figured this was a chance for him to start partying with the older kids. He paused for an instant, surprised that the bottle didn't feel cold in his hand like he thought it would, then raised it toward his mouth. As he was about to take a sip, a raw stench made him jerk the bottle away from his face, causing some of the liquid to splash onto the floor.

Curt and Randy howled, slapping their legs and rocking back and forth.

Billy set the bottle on the half wall and looked down at his clothes to make sure he hadn't spilled anything on himself.

Randy kept laughing, his mouth stretched wide, but Curt acted surprised. "Oh *shit*," he said, "that must be the bottle we was using to piss in." His face darkened. "You got something to say about it?"

Billy felt his cheeks burning as he stepped off the patio.

"That's what I thought," Curt said. "You're still such a fucking pussy, you know that?"

Doing his best not to hurry, Billy headed down the driveway, refusing to look back as Curt called after him to run on home to his mama. He couldn't help remembering to when he was ten years old and how Curt, friends with the older boys in Billy's neighborhood, would show up for pickup games of football or to shoot hoops. He'd punch Billy in the chest when he dropped a pass or missed a lay-up. He'd swat the back of his head and call him *pussy boy*. Worse were the stares from the other kids the times Billy got mad and cried in front of everyone. All to the delight of Curt.

Billy continued along the sidewalk, barely paying attention to where he was throwing his papers. Twice, mulling over what had happened with Curt—and stewing that he hadn't said or done anything to take up for himself—he accidentally skipped a house and had to backtrack. At last, though, he made it to the end of the street.

His final delivery on Altamont was a dumpy, unpainted house surrounded by a large, overgrown yard. Billy always imagined that years before, back when Brookford was nothing but sprawling countryside, the old place had been part of a big farm. Maybe the servants' quarters or something like that. It wasn't difficult to picture: There were wooden shacks among the trees behind the house, and Billy had seen chickens scurrying around in the side yard. He rarely saw the sullen-looking couple who lived there, or their young kids, none of whom ever smiled or greeted him. They paid their bill at the newspaper office downtown, which was okay with Billy since that meant he didn't have to collect from them. But an old white-haired man lived there too. The grandfather, Billy figured. He often sat on the front porch, and whenever he saw Billy, he would call hello or tell him what a fine young fellow he was.

Standing shy of the front yard, partially blocked from view behind a telephone pole, Billy saw the old man sitting in his chair as usual. After his run-in with Curt, he didn't feel like making small talk with anyone. Keeping his head down, he beelined toward the house pretending not to notice the man, planning to toss the paper onto the porch steps and walk away as quickly as he could.

"Bring that newspaper up here, would you?" the man

called, just as Billy had covered the distance and was reaching into his delivery bag.

"Dammit," he whispered to himself as he trotted up the steps.

The man had a TV tray set up in front of him on the porch. Billy laid a folded paper on it, next to a pack of Camels and a small Slurpee cup filled with butts and ashes.

"Boy, you're a quick one today," the man said. "Mister jack rabbit."

"Yes, sir," Billy said. He smiled and turned back toward the stairs.

"Hold on," the man said. "Sit down here a minute." He pointed beside him to a legless couch covered with a bedsheet. "I wanna talk to a polite young man like you."

Billy stepped closer to the TV tray but stayed on his feet. The man's speech was slurred—Billy had never noticed him sounding this way before—and he smelled of liquor and cigarettes. The undershirt he wore was spotted with food stains. For a moment, Billy felt sorry for the poor old guy.

"Have it your own way then," the man said when he saw that Billy wasn't going to take a seat. "But I got something I been meaning to ask you, and I want you to tell me the truth."

Billy suspected that he was about to get caught in the kind of small talk he'd hoped to avoid. "All right," he said.

"Here's what I wanna know," the man said, holding up a finger for Billy's full attention. "You think I'm okay, don't you?"

"Uh, I guess," Billy said. "Yes, sir."

Grinning, the man reached across the TV tray and took a loose hold of Billy's wrist. Billy stiffened but thought it might be impolite to pull away.

"Well, I think *you're* okay," the man said. "How 'bout that? I seen you walking by here every day, and I wanted you to know." He glanced toward the front door of the house and lowered his voice. "And I was thinking, if you and me wanted to be together, why, that'd be okay too, wouldn't it?"

Billy didn't understand.

"We don't gotta tell no one," the man said. "We just strip naked on a bed of mine out back."

Billy yanked his arm free. His newspaper sack swung against the TV tray as he turned, knocking it over onto the man's lap. He stared briefly at the cigarette butts and ashes covering the man's shirt and pants, then bolted across the porch and down the steps.

"What the hell's the matter with you?" the old man shouted. "You come back here to me!"

Billy started across the field next to the old man's house, running at first before slowing to a fast walk. He glanced over his shoulder. What if someone had seen him talking to the old man or, worse, had seen the man touching him— holding his hand? What if Curt was hiding somewhere, waiting to jump him, and had overheard everything? He'd laugh his ass off and tell everyone at school.

On the far side of the field was Lee-Jackson Avenue again, a quick block from Billy's drop-off point. He turned up the sidewalk, but at the Monarch Drive corner—he could tell even before he reached it—his second stack of newspapers was gone. His brick lay on the ground, broken into a couple of large chunks. He dropped his delivery sack onto the sidewalk. Curt had stolen the papers, he was sure of it. Or Curt and Randy. Who else would it be? One of them, passing by one day, had probably noticed how he stupidly left his stack sitting there. And now they'd snuck by him and taken the papers while he was on the old man's porch.

Billy took a seat on the stone wall, hating that tears were spilling onto his cheeks despite his furious attempt to hold them back. He'd go home and tell his parents everything, that's what he'd do. They'd call Curt's parents and bust him good. And they'd call the police too and have that old man locked up forever. That old pervert.

For a long while, he sat there, swiping his shirt sleeve across his face, trying to get control of himself. For once he was glad to be invisible to the people driving by, staring straight ahead in their cars, paying him no attention. Only when he'd finally calmed down and was sure he'd completely quit crying did he slide off the wall. He grabbed up his bag and set off down the hill. As Brookford's downtown came into view, though, something occurred to him. He stopped, thinking for a moment, then turned and headed back down Monarch.

Three-quarters of the way along the street, he cut through Colonel Reese's yard to the woods behind the house. He crept between the tall, Christmassy-smelling pines, careful not to slip on any moss-covered stones hidden beneath clumps of fern. As he started to emerge on the other side, he saw with satisfaction that he was directly in back of the Ralstons' house, where he figured he'd be. His papers were on the patio floor, in two piles next to the picnic-table bench.

Just then the screen door from the house to the patio swung open. Billy dropped flat to the ground, fortunately missing stones and instead landing on a soft bed of pine needles and black, spongy soil. Raising his head, he saw Randy shuffle across the patio, pause to exhale an enormous cloud of smoke, and veer down the driveway to the sidewalk. Billy waited until Randy was out of sight before hurrying behind the Ralstons' backyard toolshed, where he brushed himself off. Then he snuck further toward the house.

When he got close to the patio, he heard the stereo inside the house blaring "Cat Scratch Fever," and Curt wailing along with it. He noticed that although the screen door had closed behind Randy, the main door was wide open. As he'd hoped, the bottle of pee was still on the cinder-block half wall where he'd left it. It took him only seconds to duck across the patio, gather up the papers, and carry them around the wall to the front yard. He stuffed the papers into his sack and snuck over to the next-door neighbors' house, where he hid the sack under their front hedge.

Back on the front-yard side of the wall a minute later, kneeling in the grass, he reached above him and grabbed the bottle. He leaned it against the base of the wall and took a slow breath, trying to kill the butterflies in his stomach. Music was still blasting inside the house—Kiss's "Rock and Roll All Nite" was playing now—but he couldn't hear Curt anymore. He wondered if he shouldn't just head on home after all, but immediately shook off the feeling. With a final deep breath, and ducking low again, he got up, went and pounded on the flimsy metal frame of the patio's screen door, and raced back to his spot. The music switched off and Curt stomped through the house.

Crouching behind the half wall, Billy squeezed the bottle, his thumb covering the opening. He tried not to think about what was sloshing around inside it and breathed through his mouth to avoid the horrible smell. As soon as he heard the screen door open, he stood and threw the bottle hard, deciding at the very last second to send it flying across the floor rather than trying to bean Curt with it. It bounced once before smashing into pieces when it struck the brick next to the door, showering piss and glass everywhere. Curt was barefoot and leapt back into the house like a scared little pre-schooler. Who was the pussy boy now?

But then Curt lunged through the doorway. Billy had figured he'd easily run away before Curt, stunned by the surprise attack, could do anything about it. Instead, Curt was around the half wall in no time and only steps behind Billy, who sprinted across the front yard, around the other end of the house, and into the backyard again.

Curt got close enough to Billy to bat at his shirttail, swearing between breaths that he was going to kill him. When he made a final grab for him, though, his feet slipped out from under him and he crashed into the side of the metal toolshed.

Billy kept going, flying the rest of the way across the backyard and into the pines. But remembering his newspapers, he quit running and looked back. Curt was just getting up, cussing loudly. As Billy squatted low, a black pickup truck turned into the driveway from the street. It rumbled up beside the patio and skidded to a stop, and the man inside shouted and blew the horn. Curt said something back, just before the engine shut off. The man got out, slamming the door. "I said get your ass over here *now*," he called, his voice clear in the sudden quiet.

Hoping to see Curt get into trouble, Billy crawled closer to the yard, out of breath but ready to run away once more if he had to. Between the trees, he saw Curt limp over to the tall, thick-necked man wearing boots and mud-spattered work clothes. His crewcut was the same bright red as Curt's hair. "What the hell's going on here?" the man said.

Curt stared at the ground. "Nothin', Daddy."

His father smacked him in the face. "Don't lie to me."

"C'mon now, Daddy, *don't*," Curt said, raising a hand to shield himself.

"I come home for *my* beer, and you've already done stole it and drank it?" his father said. He popped Curt on the side of the head, then shot his arm toward the piss and broken glass. "And what's this goddam mess?"

Curt glanced to where his father pointed. When he didn't answer right away, his father hit him again, knocking him onto the patio floor.

Billy didn't move at first, his heart pumping so fast he felt dizzy and sick to his stomach. Then, as quietly as he could, he took a few steps deeper into the woods before sneaking into the next-door neighbors' backyard and around to the front. He could hear Curt bawling. As he slid his newspaper sack from under the hedge, Curt's father shouted again. Billy started looking around for a rock or a big stick—but what was his plan going to be if he actually found one or the other?

Not knowing what else to do, he shouldered his bag and, sneaking again, went over to the Ralstons' front door. He hesitated but then pressed the buzzer, causing a noise throughout the house like a telephone ringing. The sounds from the patio stopped. Billy took four or five steps back as heavy boots came tromping through the house. The door opened, and behind the screen stood Curt's father, even taller and more massive than he'd appeared outside. "Yeah, what is it?" he said, his big face greasy with sweat.

"Uh, is Curt home?" Billy said. "He was going to help me with my route."

Curt's father worked his jaw as he looked Billy up and down. "Not today he's not. He's got things to do *here*," he said, before stalking back into the room. Seconds later, the patio's screen door banged open and shut. "Curt, I ain't got time for this horseshit," Billy heard him say. "Clean this up before I'm back or I'll kill you." The truck's engine fired, and Billy heard its tires crunching gravel. It rumbled down the driveway and turned onto the street.

Billy went out to the sidewalk, watching the house until Curt appeared, a dark shape behind the front-door screen. "What are *you* lookin' at?" he said to Billy. "You the one started it all."

Billy didn't answer. He kept his eye on Curt until Curt mumbled something and closed the door. Then Billy walked along Altamont toward Lee-Jackson Avenue and home. At the end of the street, he passed the dumpy house again, trying at first not to glance at it. But when the man peered over his porch railing, Billy stared him down. The man was old, and Billy smiled at the thought that he would probably be dead soon.

Fantasy Chix

Bill Patterson waits while Jackie the realtor tries the key a third time. She jams it into the slot and jiggles it violently when it still refuses to turn. "This is so damn ridiculous," she says, leaning into the door with her shoulder. For the briefest moment, a look passes over her face that says she's had enough, to hell with it. But then, on the fourth try, the lock releases at last with a satisfying *click*. Jackie smiles and swings the door open, inviting Bill to enter the apartment ahead of her.

"Oh yes, look at *this*," Jackie says as she follows Bill into the living room. "You certainly could live it up here." He turns to see her starting down a hallway. "Fireplace in the master bedroom!" she calls a moment later.

Bill winces at the slight reek of mildew and the yellowing window curtains. The windows themselves are smudged and dirty. He peers into the kitchen and see that it's galley-style, not eat-in. On the plus side, though, the place does seem roomy. And it's open and bright. Despite the grimy windowpanes, sunlight floods the big living room, reflecting off the glossy hardwood floors. Bill has to admit that the apartment is nicer than the others he's seen so far. Besides, he's sick of searching. His recent separation from his wife, Nora, has him worn down to nothing. Not to mention having to stay with one of his brother's friends from college, week after week on a blow-up mattress, while the friend's buddies swing by every couple of nights to drink and smoke into the wee hours.

Trailing as far behind Jackie and her sales-pitch chatter as he can, Bill makes a circuit through the apartment. He clicks his fingernails on the plaster walls (all in need of fresh paint), kicks at the shoe moulding in the two bedrooms (the smaller one would work as an office), opens up the faucet in the bath (decent water pressure), then catches up with Jackie back in the living room.

"You'd have the entire second floor," she says, scanning the information sheet attached to her clipboard. "My lord, there's close to a thousand square feet total. And the rent is only twelve hundred. That's *cheap* for this neighborhood." She arches her brows, precise semicircles that appear to have been drawn on with a crayon—burnt umber, maybe, or raw sienna.

"Jackie, come on," Bill says. "You can't seriously call twelve hundred dollars cheap." Back in Brookford, three hours away, similar apartments go for less than a quarter of that. He knows the comparison isn't valid, especially having lived in the city for years, but the cost-of-living discrepancies still aggravate him.

"The market is crazy right now, hon," Jackie says. "I'm telling you, this is a good deal." She looks him hard in the eye before turning to her clipboard again. "Anyway, there's a dentist's office downstairs that should be closed at night and on the weekends. A young, single fellow lives alone on the top floor, right above us. My assistant got his name: Frank Cariello." She flips the top sheet of paper over. "So there you go. With the good doctor gone on the weekends, you and Frank can par-*tay*."

As she rattles off more stats about the building and the neighborhood—conveniently close to downtown and his office—Bill goes to one of the windows facing the street and swipes a finger across its upper pane. Directly below him, on the sidewalk in front of the building, stands a young couple, no older than sixteen or seventeen. Kelly-green spikes poke out from the boy's scalp, so bright and colorful that his torn black jacket and drab T-shirt look unimaginative in comparison. The girl wears skin-tight pink, and she's wrapped dozens of fashion chains around her waist and wrists. Both kids squint up toward Bill.

"Hello, little punks," he murmurs. Then he sees what's caught their attention: on the narrow window ledge, a large clump of gray feathers over bones the color of rotting teeth. A dead pigeon, its leg somehow caught under the closed window.

Bill unlocks the window and opens it, but the bird doesn't move. A black pool of dried blood keeps its crumpled foot glued in place. "How the *hell*?" he says. Did the idiot who shut the window not notice the bird? Didn't anyone hear it shrieking?

Jackie walks over. "What is it?"

Bill inches the window up further, but it doesn't hold. It slams shut with a heavy thud. The bird drops out of sight, then plops onto the sidewalk at the couple's feet. The boy leaps back, sticking up his middle finger and jabbing it like an ice pick in Bill's direction. "Fuck you, you fuck!" he shouts. He grabs an empty can out of the gutter and flings it at the window. It hits the brick below the ledge. The girl gives Bill the finger as well, before hooking her boyfriend by the collar of his jacket and towing him along the sidewalk.

"Up yours too," Jackie mutters as the teenagers disappear down the street.

Bill stares at her. "Did that just happen?"

"You better believe it, hon. Never a dull moment." She grins. "You wouldn't want it any other way, would you?"

⁜

Bill signs a lease and moves in the following Saturday. As agreed, the landlord has changed the front-door lock, and the new key works like a charm. He has also had the apartment painted—unfortunately, a cheap job with some sort of industrial-strength paint that smells vaguely to Bill like a mix of sweet, overripe peaches and unwashed feet. And the windows are still dirty. And the floors need cleaning. He goes from room to room with a bottle of Windex, a roll of paper towels, and a sponge mop as the movers cart his belongings in.

The movers—"Two Chucks, One Truck"—ignore Bill's Magic Marker scrawls on his containers. After they leave the apartment early that evening, with four hundred dollars of Bill's cash in their pockets, he discovers three big boxes clearly labeled "Kitchen" stacked in the bathtub. Maybe they can't read? He decides to call them "Two Major Assholes, One Truck." And when he notices—how did he not notice earlier?—that they've buried his mattress under crates of books and CDs and old record albums in the living room, he considers calling the Better Business Bureau. But right away he laughs at the idea. "The Better Business Bureau? Yeah, right." He points at his reflection in a tall mirror that's leaning against the wall. "*You* are a *dork*."

He throws open the living room windows to draw in the early October air and sees the blood stain again and what's left of the poor pigeon's crushed leg. He'd almost forgotten about it. After propping the window open with a small box so it doesn't slam shut again, he takes out the Windex and scrubs the ledge. The leg comes up, but he can't remove the stain completely. So he resigns himself to living with it, imagining it a sort of birthmark, a reminder of everything he's gone through to enter this new stage of his life.

✧✧✧

Bill and Nora have been separated for two months. Bill tries not to think about it, but he can't help replaying everything over and over in his mind, especially at night when he's alone, as he is now.

It was late July, and Nora's parents were visiting from Turnersburg, just up the road from Brookford. Bill and Nora always marveled that though they'd come from small towns not thirty minutes from each other, both involved in typical small-town activities growing up—paper route, YMCA swim team, summer jobs at the Dairy Queen and the mall—they'd met and fallen in love only after moving away from that life, to the "big city" hours north. They were both now happy—proud—to call themselves city dwellers. In fact, before Nora's parents arrived, Nora acted excited, manic almost, and talked on and on about "showing off the nabe" to Wendy and Dick.

At first, the weekend proceeded along fine. On Friday night, they ordered Vietnamese take-out, and except for Dick's comment about "all the godforsaken nut jobs in this city of yours," the conversation was pleasant enough. Nora's parents asked about Bill's job at the marketing firm and praised Nora's interior design skills. "I love what y'all have done with this place, sweetie. I don't know where you get your sophisticated taste, but it sure doesn't come from me," Wendy said. She laughed but then appeared a little put out when no one contradicted her.

On Saturday, they hiked. Up the boulevard to the war memorial, across the park for lemonade and TCBY frozen yogurt, through the kaleidoscopic stalls of the farmers' market, and on to the natural history museum. Bill was happy to let Nora and her parents walk several steps ahead, sharing news about relatives and hometown friends. Occasionally, Nora would glance back and stretch a hand toward Bill. He'd take it, and the four of them would stroll along quietly. Bill couldn't remember feeling more content.

They drove to Ashland Lake on Sunday, one of the scenic recreational areas west of the city, and found a secluded stretch of sand for a picnic. The day was hot, cloudlessly blue and bright. They all wore bathing suits, but no one ventured into the water. After lunch, though—a pass-around feast of deviled eggs, pimento cheese and fresh bread, and slices of ripe watermelon—Nora's parents did set off on what they said would be a long jaunt, hoping to make it to the paddle-boat rental shed, a good mile along the shore.

Five minutes after they'd left, Nora snuggled next to Bill on the blanket he was stretched out on. She pulled a pink beach towel over the both of them and kissed Bill on the mouth. "Should we, *you* know?" she said, reaching between his legs.

He propped himself up on his elbows. "Here?" He glanced around and saw that they were well hidden, with thick woods behind them and gray, neglected-looking picnic tables on either side. "You know me, I'm up for anything, but—"

"I'm feeling *wild* for some reason," she said, and kissed him harder.

Bill closed his eyes, but opened them when Nora pulled away suddenly. Tears had filled her eyes and were beginning to spill over her lashes. "What's wrong?" he said.

She brought her fingertips to his cheeks. "I just, um, love

you so much," she said, trying to smile. Then she wiped her nose on the back of her hand and stood up. "You're right, this is crazy. I should catch up with my folks and make sure they don't dawdle."

"Wait a sec," Bill said. But she was already bolting across the sand.

Nora didn't say much after she and her parents returned from their walk. She was quiet on the drive back to the apartment too. Bill guessed that she was just tired, probably a little overwhelmed being around her family for two days straight.

As soon as they got home, Nora announced that she needed a good soak and disappeared. When she came into the living room an hour later, fresh from the bath but with splotchy cheeks and red-rimmed eyes, she stood behind the sofa, where her parents were spread out, sharing sections of the newspaper. Bill sat in the rocker on the other side of the room, working the Sunday crossword.

"Everything okay, sugar?" Dick asked Nora over his shoulder.

"I don't know, but . . . I've come to a decision," she said. "I think Bill and I need a break. Um, a separation."

"What are you talking about?" Bill said.

Nora's face fell and she looked to her parents without answering. Then Wendy and Dick were coming around the sofa and draping their arms around her.

Bill pushed himself out of his chair. "Nora!" But she and her parents were already heading down the hall to the bedroom.

+‡+

At this point in his remembering, Bill's brain seems to overload and power down. All it allows are quick, fleeting images, like a video being fast-forwarded. Nora weeping and saying, "I don't know *why* I feel this way." Bill stomping around in the hall outside their bedroom, threatening to throw their wedding china into the dumpster. His little brother, who had moved back to Brookford after graduating from college in the city, helpfully wondering aloud on the phone days later whether Nora was a "lesbo."

Even now, cut off from his wife and set up in a new apartment of his own, Bill doesn't understand all of Nora's reasons for wanting to split up. Doesn't understand why she came on to him at the lake that day. Was she trying to convince herself that she still had feelings for him? Did she ever truly have feelings for him at all?

"Maybe she *is* a lesbo!" he shouts. He closes the windows, then takes the crates off the mattress and curls himself on top of it. When he wakes up, it's two in the morning. The living room's overhead light is still on, shining as brightly as it did hours earlier. Bill stares into it, whispers, "Fuck you, you fuck," and drifts back into troubled sleep.

The next day begins for Bill the same way every other day has begun for him the past two months, with a flu-like achiness as he needles himself with mental snapshots of Nora in bed with someone else. The someone is no one in particular, although Bill imagines, despite his brother's comment, a male Olympian: six-foot-five, with pecs and biceps as hard as marble. Nora wags her hips and humps away as she never humped with Bill. She's completely naked. Or her valentine-red panties are around her ankles and she's wearing a skimpy top—a slutty, silver-lamé number she's been dying to parade around in now that Bill's out of the picture. Or she's bent over the kitchen sink with only an apron on, and that son of a bitch *someone* is taking her from behind.

Groaning, Bill forces his thoughts elsewhere. To Nora on their wedding day, gliding toward him down the aisle. The day they drove out into the countryside near Turnersburg during a trip home, cruising along with the windows wide open, Nora's cornsilk hair blowing all around and making them both laugh so hard that Bill almost crashed into a guardrail. Their first date. Their first awkward kiss, under a crippled umbrella in the freezing rain.

But for Bill, now alone, these memories are worse than the pornographic images. He lets his head drop over the edge of the mattress and catches himself in the mirror again. "Stop," he pleads. "Just stop it."

The one thing that's given him a respite from this self-torture is work, anything that keeps him busy. He rubs his eyes and sits up. Glancing around at the mountains of bags and cartons and crates and bins, he feels a tiny bit of relief.

⊹⊹

By day seven, Bill has made some headway. Although the second bedroom/office is still filled with knick-knacks and furniture, and unpacked boxes are stacked in every corner of the master bedroom, there is virtually no clutter in the living room.

On Friday night, Bill comes home from work at eight, grabs a Heineken out of the refrigerator, and plants himself on his cranberry-colored futon sofa. Nora laid claim to the nice, expensively upholstered couch her parents had given them. No one has tried to reach him on his work phone today, and he sees now that he hasn't received any calls here either: His answering machine sits on the glass coffee table with no message light blinking. He pulls hard from his beer.

He goes to his computer, which he's set up on a card table by the pigeon-stain window until the office is cleared out. Checks his e-mail. Nothing. No mail, of course, from Nora. God forbid she would take five minutes out of her life to make sure he was back in one piece after she buzz-sawed him off at the knees. And nothing from his parents or brother. No *How ya doing? . . . Hang in there . . . We love you.*

The only contact Bill has had with his family since moving, in fact, was a phone call to Brookford on Tuesday night. He'd simply wanted to give his parents his new home number. Quick, painless. But his mother couldn't help herself. As soon as his father handed the phone over to her, she said, "Billy, honey, I've been thinking. I know your brother shouldn't have said it the way he did, but *could* Nora be a gay?"

"A *gay*? Mom, I can't even imagine how to respond to that."

They haven't talked since.

Bill takes a few more sips from his beer before guz-

zling the rest of it and fetching another. He goes back to
the computer and stares at the screen. Wonders who, other
than family and Nora, he can call or e-mail. Although occasionally in touch with old Brookford friends, as well as a
couple of guys he knew in college, as an adult he's never had
a real buddy, someone he can just ring up, night or day, to
shoot the proverbial shit with. Someone to hang out with
or—at times like this—to help keep his mind from racing
full-throttle into panic mode.

Fifteen minutes later, a car door slams shut in front of the
building. Bill peers out the window in time to see a white
taxi pull away from the curb. On the sidewalk, surrounded
by a small city of big, blocky suitcases, a young guy fumbles
to pull keys out of his pocket. Bill wondered when he would
meet his neighbor; the upstairs apartment has been quiet every night this week.

The building's main door opens and closes and the guy
trots up the stairs, singing "O sole mio, I got to pee-o!" in
a loud, echoing baritone. Maybe he has a sense of humor.
Bill remembers this same silly rhyme from when he was in
elementary school.

The floorboards creak overhead as the guy hurries
through his apartment. Bill waits a moment, then heads
downstairs and outside. He hoists two of the suitcases and
starts back up. His neighbor meets him halfway, on the
landing outside Bill's.

"Who the fuck are you?" the guy says, his heavy eyebrows coming together in a black, batlike V.

Bill sets the bags down, bristling at the guy's question. "I'm Bill, your new neighbor," he says. "I thought you could use some help, but maybe I was wrong."

"Help?" the guy says, with a smartass grin. "We don't need no stinkin' help." His arms are at his sides. In one hand, he holds a shiny pistol against his black overcoat.

Bill's jaw goes slack, and he takes a step backward. The guy cocks his head to one side, then laughs when he sees what Bill is looking at. "Yo, false alarm, dude," he says. "I was just fuckin' with you. Didn't mean to scare the shit outta you, you know?"

Bill stares at the guy, no idea how to respond.

The guy brings the handgun up in front of his face. Its chrome plating reflects the hallway's dim lighting, but Bill sees that its short barrel is plugged with a red plastic stopper. The guy squeezes the trigger, the gun pops, and a hot sulfur smell fills the hall, as though firecrackers have been set off. "Fuckin' cap gun. Was foolin' around with it in the cab."

Bill manages a slight nod.

"Anyway, I'm Kee," the guy says.

Bill isn't sure he's heard right. "Kee?"

"As in 'Frank-*kee*,'" the guy says. "How my mother used to call me. Name just stuck, you know?"

⁜

An hour later, Bill and Kee are lounging on the overstuffed leather couches in Kee's living room. Drinking beer, eating pizza delivered from Jo-Jo Junior's around the corner. "Best on the fuckin' East Coast," Kee says through a mouthful of mozzarella.

It turns out that Kee travels a lot as a sales rep for his family's business. "Italian stuff: specialty items and kitchen shit," he says. "My old man sends me all over the place, you know? All over the states, I mean. Would love to go to ol' Europa, but so far, no deal." He bites into a fresh slice, sucks loudly through his puckered lips, and throws his head back to keep his long, thick hair out of the cheese and sauce.

In spite of the bizarre cap-gun incident, Kee seems all right. He likes to talk, and Bill relaxes listening to him. As he rambles on about his work and travels, Bill takes everything in. Kee's expensive-looking clothes, all black. His spit-polished Kenneth Coles. The apartment décor: blood-red walls, sleek chrome tables and mahogany bookcases, framed movie posters everywhere. *The Godfather, Scarface, Taxi Driver.*

Bill also notices, on the bottom shelf of one of the bookcases, a collection of Hemingway hardcover editions kept upright by a tall stack of magazines. A *Hustler* is on top. Kee is a man's man *and* a lady's man. Probably has lots of buddies—and lots of girlfriends. Bill imagines all the creaking and thumping he'll be hearing overhead from now on. But what kind of guy displays his porn collection out in the open like this? Then again, it seems appropriate for Kee.

After finishing his second beer and his third slice of pizza, Bill excuses himself to use the bathroom. As he heads down the hall, Kee calls after him, "So what's your deal?"

"Uh, my wife and I are separated. I'm basically just trying to figure out where I go from here." Bill shakes his head and tells himself to shut up.

In the bathroom, he spies more magazines tucked under the sink—another *Hustler* and one with a fluorescent pink cover called *Fantasy Chix*. After washing up, he picks up the *Fantasy Chix* and flips the shiny pages.

Kee calls again from the living room, "How long you guys been split up?"

"Couple months," Bill calls back. He turns the magazine sideways for a better look at the redhead sporting nothing but retro-style skates and a gold roller-derby helmet.

"So which one of you was cheating, you know? Screwin' around."

"It wasn't like that," Bill says, his pulse pounding as he checks out the two lesbians with pirate hats and eye patches going at it on a desert isle. He can't help but think of Nora.

"Oh, yeah?" Kee says. "What *was* it like?"

Bill has turned to the phone sex ads in the back of the magazine. Many, to his surprise, list local city numbers. Before he can answer Kee, his eye catches something and he feels as if he's been punched in the gut. Under a boldfaced heading that reads "Call mmmMoi," a young woman lies naked on a heart-shaped bed, legs spread, a phone to her ear. She looks just like Nora.

"Yo," Kee says. "Did you fall in or what, dude?"

Bill ignores him. He holds the page three inches from his nose, racking his brain.

He met Nora only six months before they got married. About all she would say of her post-Turnersburg life was that she moved to the city right after high school to try modeling. When that didn't work out, she took three or four classes at one of the city universities but never completed a degree. She also went through a wild phase at one time. "A promiscuous phase," as she put it. Bill never liked the sound of that, but whenever he asked Nora about it, she would get weepy and say, "I love you *now*. I don't care about the past. I never—*ever*—think about all that." She'd flick her wrist as if swatting *all that* away.

But phone sex? Porn ads? Bill can't believe she would've been caught up in something like that. And yet, here she is.

He lays the magazine open on the back of the toilet and quietly searches the bathroom. In the medicine cabinet above the sink, he finds a pack of razor blades and extracts one. He draws the blade down the inside seam of the page and gently tears it away, then folds it and slides it into his back pocket.

"Dude?" It's Kee again. Closer this time, outside the door. "You aren't blowing chunks, are you?" His voice is pinched and angry. "That would *not* be cool."

Bill flushes the toilet, returns the blade to its place, and pulls the door open. "Just checking out your reading material." He holds up the magazine.

Kee's eyes are stony, his mouth a rigid line. When he sees the *Fantasy Chix,* though, he gives Bill an evil grin. "Jerkin' the turkey, huh? Wouldn't blame you if you did. Couple of beauties in there, you know?"

Bill grits his teeth, afraid he might blow chunks after all. He tosses the magazine back under the sink.

"Dude, we need to hit a few places," Kee says. "Get you back in the swing, you know? Get you *laid*."

Bill wants to be alone so that he can get a better look at the photo. "I'm definitely not ready for that," he says.

"Whatever. But I'm sure your ex ain't waitin' around to get back out there."

And all at once, there it is. Bill didn't truly believe it—didn't want to believe it—even as he tortured himself with his X-rated images of Nora. But hearing Kee say it so plainly confirms it for him. Of *course* she's out there. Of *course* she's hoping to meet someone—if she isn't seeing somebody already.

"You're right," Bill says, staring at the floor for a moment before raising his head and looking Kee in the eye. "Let's fucking *go*."

⊹⊹⊹

They decide to meet up again at eleven thirty. Back in his apartment, Bill examines the *Fantasy Chix* photo, studying it under every light and lamp in his place. Finally, he slips it into his pocket again and cracks another beer.

"So what if it *is* her," he says. But who is he kidding? "Shit!" If the guy hadn't left his stupid porn lying around.

In Bill's mind, the image of Nora the porn star morphs into Kee the psycho neighbor. What was his problem outside the bathroom? If a long trip to the toilet makes him angry, who knows what else might set him off?

⁘

In the taxi, Kee cranes his neck forward to get a look out the front windshield. "Friday night at Zooma is *wild*, you know? Been horny for this all week." His hair is slicked back, and he smells as though he's been body-surfing in the Musk Oil Sea. Bill breathes through his mouth and tries not to talk. Occasionally, he takes a pull from one of the beers Kee has brought along for the ride.

They drive to a neighborhood of lofts and warehouses near the river called Shackenbach, or "Shake and Bake" as most people refer to it, in honor of the area's drug-fueled club scene. The sidewalks are packed with neo-punks and neo-hippies, drag queens and preppy frat boys, yuppies and pacifier-sucking ravers.

Bill's never been much of a partygoer. Nora usually had to beg and cajole just to get him out for the occasional drink or dinner with friends. He's never been to a dance club before. He figured a big one called Zooma would advertise itself with klieg lights and a neon banner. But as he steps from the car, all he sees is a dimly lit loading bay beneath a renovated warehouse. Bass-heavy electronic music rocks the building. At the back of the bay, two bouncers stand on a platform behind a velvet rope. The line to get beyond the rope and the bouncers stretches around the block.

"Don't worry about it," Kee says. "They know me here."

Sure enough, one of the bouncers, a dough-faced Uncle

Fester lookalike, unclips the rope and allows Kee and Bill to slip to one side of the line. He blows Kee a kiss as they go through the curtained entrance. "Kiki doll!" he says, his hyper-thyroidal eyes bulging.

"Yeah-yeah, in your dreams," Kee calls over his shoulder as the curtains close behind them.

At the end of a long, ebony-walled corridor, they turn a corner and the club's high-ceilinged, cavernous main room opens before them. Bill had expected something similar to a high-school dance: a lone mirror ball rotating above a darkened gym floor. But here, there are mirror balls everywhere he looks. And spotlights and strobes and lasers. All spinning and jabbing in time to the insistent *thump thump thump* of the music, which is a hundred times louder than it was on the street and in the corridor. Above the sound of the music is the noise of the crowd and the hiss of the fog machines that blow dense white clouds throughout the room. On one wall three stories high, thousands of colored lights blink and flash. They spell out "ZOOMA!" as a rocket ship launches and then explodes in a burst of crimson and orange and purple.

"Woo-*hoo*!" Kee shouts. "This way, dude."

Bill stands motionless for a moment, enjoying the intense excitement of the club, before hurrying to catch up with Kee. He follows him across the main floor, through the vast expanse of wiggling, writhing bodies. No one is dancing with a partner. From what Bill can tell, everyone simply sways and gyrates and humps with whoever's closest.

Bill dodges and weaves to avoid smashing into anyone. The crowd looks about the same as the one on the sidewalks, except there's much more exposed flesh here. Shirtless, muscle-bound steroid addicts. Lean, long-limbed women in skin-tight leggings and scanty black-lace tops. Feline go-go dancers wearing next to nothing inside giant metal birdcages suspended from the ceiling.

Bill and Kee reach the far wall and the cave-like bar carved into it. "Six Zooma-kazes," Kee calls to the skinny Goth bartender. "Line 'em up!" He slaps down a hundred-dollar bill and turns to Bill. "House drink. Basically just *huge* kamikazes, you know? I'll get this round."

In seconds, six oversized margarita glasses sparkle in front of them, each brimming with icy, pale-green liquid.

"Two to flip, one to sip," Kee says before downing the first in one shot. "Go for it!"

Bill takes the second glass by the stem and brings the drink under his nose. It's sweet. Sickly sweet. Already feeling half drunk and bloaty from the numerous beers he's put away, he manages only a small gulp.

"C'mon, straight back," Kee says. "Zoo-*ma*! Zoo-*ma*!"

Bill takes a breath and polishes off the rest of the drink. He slides the empty glass back to its place in line, shivering as the vodka and lime juice burn inside him.

Kee throws back the next Zooma-kaze with ease. He sets the glass down, picks up the fourth, and points toward the remaining two. "All yours."

Bill raises the next glass to his lips, pauses for an instant, then snaps his head back, surprised at how easy the drink goes down this time. "Whew!" he says, smiling. He lifts his final drink and clinks glasses with Kee.

As they stand sipping, Bill grins as a pleasant exhilaration washes over him. Watching the go-go dancers, he's reminded of the *Fantasy Chix* page in his pocket. But that seems so stupid now. He suddenly wants to tell Kee about the picture and Nora and the fact that she might be a lesbian and how freaking ridiculous the entire situation is now that he really thinks about it. He opens his mouth to speak, but Kee has disappeared. He glances back at Goth, who nods toward the dance floor. Bill turns to see Kee wading in, hands fisted above his head, pelvis pumping. His eyes meet Bill's for an instant just as he's swallowed into the crowd.

Bill sips his Zooma-kaze for another minute, then drains the rest of it and starts after Kee. But his path is blocked. He sees paisley-patterned tights and a navy, bikini-looking top. His eyes linger on the woman's chest. Her hands go to her hips.

"Are you drunk?" she says, her high-pitched voice piercing the club noise.

"I am getting *wasted*!" he says proudly, then stares into her squinched-up face. He recognizes the face. It's Patsy, one of Nora's close friends.

"I guess that's *one* way to get over a breakup," she says.

Bill can't believe it. How could he wind up bumping into Patsy, of all people? At a Shake and Bake dance club, of all places? She was always so unfriendly to him, always so possessive of Nora's time and attention. Instead of feeling anger or frustration, though, Bill finds himself struck by Patsy's gorgeous brown eyes, her full pouty lips. He could never get beyond her unpleasant personality to admire how truly good-looking she was. But now . . .

"So basically, I told her she needed to quit sitting around her apartment and go have some fun." Patsy is explaining something. Something important, it seems, from the way she levels her gaze at him.

Bill nods several times before realizing he has no idea what she's talking about. "What?"

"I said I *told* her she should get out and have some fun. Did she call you or something?"

"Who?" Bill says. Then it dawns on him. "Nora?"

Patsy squinches her face again. "Uh, *yeah*. Who else would I be talking about?"

"I didn't come with her," Bill says, trying to puzzle out why she'd think that.

"Oh, that's good," Patsy says. "I mean, no offense, but that wouldn't be too smart, right?" She glances along the bar. "So who *are* you with?"

As though conjured from out of the dance-floor mist, Kee appears. His face is red and shiny with sweat. "Fuckin' crazy in there!" he says to Bill. Noticing Patsy, he reaches out his hand. "What's up? I'm Kee."

"I'm sorry?" she says, leaning in toward him.

"Kee," he says. "As in 'Frank-*Keeee*!'" He holds the note as long as he can, then whoops and howls like a coyote.

Her eyes go wide. "Okay, uh . . . Kee," she says. "I'm Patsy? A friend of Nora's?"

"Nora. My wife," Bill says to Kee. "Soon to be ex." In his drunkenness, he laughs at how his words slur together. "My *soombiex.*" He glances over his shoulder again to see if Goth is listening, but no one is behind the bar now.

When he turns back around, Kee has Patsy by the hand, leading her into the crowd. Bill wonders again about what she said. Did Nora tell Patsy she was thinking about getting in touch with him? "Wait!" he calls, wanting to ask her. But they're gone. He takes a step, then stops, swaying like someone on the deck of a ship. The swirling and twirling all around him are too fast. The music—and the people singing and shouting—is too loud. He clutches the back of a barstool, attempting to steady himself as the room spins. He closes one eye and peers toward the dance floor again. No way he's going to find them now.

⁍⁋⁍

Bill takes a cab home, feeling green and queasy the entire ride. He manages not to get sick, though, and once they reach his apartment building, he stumbles upstairs and passes out on his futon couch. For hours, he lies asleep on his back, one foot on the floor like an anchor.

In the middle of the night, he's vaguely aware of footsteps, muffled voices, and echoing laughter in the stairwell. His head pounds, and he still feels tipsy, but he sits up. He knows that laugh. It's Patsy again. Is Kee hooking up with her?

Bill gets up from the couch and sneaks to his door. Before he can crack it open, he realizes there are two female voices. Patsy and . . . Nora?

Kee's front door slams shut. Bill listens to the footsteps above him. He hears music, the same kind of electronica that was blasting at the club, then what sounds like the three of them jumping up and down in unison. Wouldn't Patsy have told Nora that Bill lives downstairs? Would Nora even care?

Bill rubs his palms down the front of his jeans and starts pacing, his head cocked toward the ceiling. He wants to run upstairs and punch Kee in the mouth. Wants to shake some sense into Nora.

Within minutes, the jumping stops. Bill still hears the music booming, but no people. He tiptoes through his apartment, barely breathing, down the hall, into the office, the bathroom. Finally his bedroom. He stands there, the hairs on the back of his neck pricking up like a thousand micro-antennas. Then he hears it. *Creak, creak, creak.* Slow. Then faster. And faster.

"Son of a bitch!"

In a panic, he grabs the broom he's left leaning against the closet door. He's about to whale away with it on the ceiling when his eye catches the fire escape railing outside his window. He crosses the room and slides the window open.

The creaking and thumping are louder. Bill crawls through the window as fast as he can, onto the iron slats of the fire escape's landing, which perches above a narrow alley beside the building. Outside, it's blustery. He's cold in his shirtsleeves but fully awake and sober now. A full moon lights his way up the escape.

At the top of the steps, he crouches and listens but hears only music coming from inside. He crawls under Kee's window and peeks over the ledge. The moon reflects off the glass, but there's a bedside lamp shining inside the room and Bill can see straight in. A girl he's never seen before, a lanky teenager wearing only a polka-dotted bra and panties, sits in a leather recliner in the corner smoking a cigarette. A nest of discarded clothes is at her feet.

On the bed, partially covered under a tangle of sheets and blankets, are the other two. Kee on top, only his shoulders and the back of his head visible; the other girl buried in shadow.

Bill rises onto his knees. He doesn't care whether they see him now. Kee looks as if he's doing push-ups. Bill's heart races; he's afraid he might pass out again. The girl rolls her head. Dark curls frame her adolescent face. It isn't Nora.

Bill ducks out of sight. He lies flat on his back under the window, waiting for his pulse to slow. After a minute, he rolls onto his stomach, crawls back to the steps, and carefully descends them. On the landing outside his own window, he pulls the glossy *Fantasy Chix* page from his pocket and unfolds it. In the light of the moon, he studies the photo. The woman's face, her thin body, the way she lifts one leg higher than the other, how she splays her fingers across her belly.

It isn't her. Bill has never been so sure of anything in his life.

Just then a strong wind gusts up through the slats of the landing, causing it to vibrate and shake. Thrown off balance, Bill lets go of the magazine page and grabs for the railing with both hands. The page gets blown high above the alley, like something come alive and taking flight. Instinctively he reaches for it, leaning out over the railing as far as he can, stretching with one hand, then the other, then—too late—realizing that he can't pull himself back. As he starts to topple over the side, his right arm catches between two of the railing's iron posts, wrenching the arm from its socket but slowing his fall. He manages to grab the base of another post with his left hand.

Hanging from the landing, barely able to hold on, he tries to pull himself up, but any movement makes his dislocated shoulder scream with pain. "Help!" he cries. He pivots just enough to spot Kee's window above. There's a shift in the light, and Kee appears at the glass with a sheet wrapped around him. "Kee!" Bill calls. But Kee might as well be an image on a television screen. He cups his hands to either side of his face and peers out, pressing his nose to the window. But he doesn't open it, doesn't lean out to investigate the sound he thinks he's heard. He steps back and lowers the shade.

"No! Kee!"

Bill continues to shout, but he's rapidly losing his grip and in so much pain he's close to tears. "What the hell were you thinking?" he says to himself. "What is your freaking problem?" He can't turn his head far enough to look up the alley toward the street, but wonders if anyone else has heard him crying out. He sees the *Fantasy Chix* page continuing to dance on the breeze, merrily swaying left and right before spiraling downward and out of sight. Twenty-five feet below him, dozens of cardboard boxes and bags of garbage are piled outside the building's basement entrance. If he could just relax for a minute and calm down, he's certain he'd be okay. Even if he has to fall onto the boxes and bags and risk breaking a bone or two, that would be all right. That would be a start.

And so, after thinking it through, after closing his eyes, counting down from five, and taking a deep breath, Bill starts by letting go.

Role Model

THE PHILOSOPHY OF WAGS

1989

Hey, everyone. Everyone? Hey. Simmer down, y'all, okay? Let's all simmer down. Yeah, can you close that window? Wait a minute. Oh my God, listen to me: "Simmer down." I *told* myself I wouldn't start off like this, and here I am already sounding like some old fart—or one of my old teachers, more like. Ms. Hauser or Mr. Goodlaw or, what's her name, Miss Byrd. Wow, it has been quite a while since I thought about her. Is she still here? Yeah? She must be, what, a hundred these days? Okay, okay, it's okay to laugh, but listen now, don't go telling her I said that. Y'all got me covered, right?

But serious now, I know I might be up here fuckin' around—oops, *damn*, I have *got* to watch that!—sorry, up here *joking* around, about high school and whatnot. But let me tell you, them ten years since I been outta school? Went by like that. I shit you not. One day you're up there at the top of the old totem pole, sneakin' smokes behind the gym, chasing pu— sorry, chasing the *girls*. I didn't say it, okay? Then they spring you loose, and can we say "real world"? Man, I am *telling* you. You don't know how good you got it right now. Enjoy it while you can.

Anyway, hey, I'm Archie Wagner. Sorry, they told me you gotta call me *Mister* Wagner. Wow, that sounds weird. I didn't write it on the board or nothing. It ain't hard—Wag. Ner. But you know what? Screw it, just call me Wags. Y'all won't tell, right?

I, uh— Hey, can you not do that? Thanks, big guy. Appreciate it.

So, I'm your sub today, filling in for, let's see . . . Ms. Patterson, yeah. She's Billy's mom, right? I knew that little guy. Wonder where he's at now. Really? Headed up to the big city, huh? That's cool. I'll have to look him up next time I take a road trip thataway.

Anyway, Billy's mom has left me, wow, all manner of notes and shit up here. Seriously, though, look at this. How'm I supposed to figure this out? Does this sound right to you? "Period one: Finish eight problems and review homework." Is that *chapter* eight or something? All right, good then. So I guess y'all should just finish the problems you been working on. I reckon you know better than me.

Huh? Oh, right. Attendance. Okay, uh, everybody here? Anybody not here? Who? Wait, let me get something to write with. *Shit.* Why the hell ain't there a frickin' pencil . . . Oh, here we go. Okay, shoot. Janette Carpenter? With a "C"? Got it, man. Thanks.

Okay, that's it. Anybody got any questions or anything? Anyone? All right, then. That's cool. I'll just sit here.

But hey, serious now, not to interrupt or anything, but watchin' y'all brings everything *right* back, you know what I mean? Wow. I remember sitting in class like you are now, working problems and whatnot, or woodshop, or runnin' laps in the gym—it don't matter what it was. And let me say, I was pretty damn pissed off, I'll tell you *that*. I can understand where you're at right now. With all there was awaitin' me out there? I figured, screw it—why'm I wasting my time inside when the big, bad world is out there passing me by? Like, there's gotta be somethin' better than Brookford. Am I right?

Well, look, I've learned different now. Y'all need to have your shit *together* out there, okay? So, don't do what I do, do what I tell you to do . . . or however that old saying goes. I'm just trying to pass on some of the knowledge and whatnot I've picked up. That's really why I'm doing this. It might sound kinda weird, but I want y'all to think of me as a role model or something. I'm serious. Someone you can look up to, or who's "been there," I guess, because—

Hey, uh, man? What's your name? Kevin? All right, Kev, well, I'm trying to be cool and all up here, but you have *got* to sit yourself down, all right? What? Come on, you should've thought about that before. You can grab it after class. Yep. I know, I know, I'm sounding like Mr. Big Boss-man-Asshole, but I think we all need to just mellow out a little bit, all right?

Anyway, what was I saying? Oh yeah, role model. That's

what I'm tryin' to do here. And the first thing is: Y'all have *got* to take control of your own, what I call, *destiny*. That is lesson one, all right? And that's a lesson I learned the hard way. Let me tell you, after high school? I was basically partying 'round the frickin' clock. Then one day I, quote-unquote, "woke up." Looked around and said, This shit ain't *workin'*. Right? I mean, serious now—and don't go blabbering about this—but laying around in your jockeys all day? Tokin' up like it's going outta style? Got the little "dealership" going, if you know what I mean? Enough to pay the bills and whatnot. Okay, go ahead and giggle your asses off, but y'all know where I'm coming from, right? Come on, you can't tell me you ain't heard worse. *Much* worse, am I right?

Anyway, I ain't proud of any of that. And I *did* take control of my destiny. Saw an opportunity and frickin' jumped, okay? Sized myself up and . . .

Except, uh, now that I'm thinking on it, I guess it was easier for *me* to jump than it might be for someone else. I mean, not to brag or nothin'—that is *not* why I'm here, okay?—but as you can see, I happen to be, I don't want to say "hot," but, you know, good-lookin' and all. And listen, I don't care what all shit they're telling you, that *does* make a difference out there. Yeah, yeah, laugh about it, but it does.

'Fact, I wasn't gonna get into all this, but, uh . . . Y'all heard about a little somethin' called Girls Nite Out? Anybody heard of them? Let's see a show of hands. So, everybody. *Cool.* All right, then.

Girls Nite is what saved my ass, if you can believe it.

Might save yours too—you never know. But you have got to be ready when something like that comes your way. Like I was. Like I said, I'm loungin' around the house, tokin' it up—*but,* the one thing I done right? Kept working out after high school, okay? Kept my weight bench, my free weights, the whole nine yards. Then one day I heard that ad on the radio. That Girls Nite Out ad? Cool, right? "Show us your stuh-uh-uff and *YOU!* can be one of uh-uh-us!"

Hey now, man, be cool. I didn't say I *could* sing. What I'm *sayin'* is, that ad was, like, a wake-up call for ol' Wags, all right? I headed down to this, uh, well it's that big-ass trailer out there on Lee-Jackson, almost at the county line. You know the one I'm talking about? Back behind that new car wash, yeah. Had a interview with Miss Scarlotta Pincus— she's part owner of Girls Nite—and she was like, "Wags, I *do* like your stuff." Her exact words. I shit you not. And next thing you know, *blam,* I'm doing my thing at a few of them, what I call, stag parties for chicks, okay? Yeah, them bachelorette party deals. That's why they call it Girls Nite Out. And—oh my God—can we say "rakin' it in"? *Rakin'.* Y'all heard of them stripper-grams up in New York City or wherever? That's what this is, only a hell of a lot cooler, 'cause instead of one chick, you got like fifteen or twenty chicks, all hollering at you so they can stuff cash down the front of your drawers.

I. Shit. You. *Not.*

Okay, okay, laugh it up, but I was the one laughing, all right? All the way to the frickin' *bank.*

What's that? You don't gotta raise your hand or nothing. No, no, I don't mean no offense here. Look, Debbie—you're Debbie, right?—when I say "chick," I mean "girl," all right? I apologize to all the ladies in class here if I offended anyone, but I'm just telling you straight. Everybody hearing this? This is real world, okay? No bullshit. Here again, I'm just trying to tell all y'all what it's like out there, you hear me?

So, uh, any-the-frickin'-way . . . *Damn*, I got off my subject line there. Didn't mean to tell y'all my life story or nothing. Huh? Yeah, I still dance some, here and there. Usually they'll rent out the VFW for a night, and I'll do my thing. Ain't a big deal. But basically I made some good money for a spell and now I'm on to a whole shitload of different stuff—like what I'm doin' here. You know? Mentoring, counseling . . . Shit like that. That's really what I wanna get into full-time. But Girls Nite Out is *definitely* something you should go for. Maybe not all of y'all, but Girls Nite does take chicks—I mean *girls*—too, so, uh . . .

What? Naw, man. No way, I ain't gonna do that. Naahh. Don't even ask, all right? No fuckin' way. I don't know, man. Really? Naw. *Really?* Y'all wanna see some of what I got? Serious now? Damn, I probably shouldn't do this, but . . . Oh, what the diddly-frick. All right then, check the hall, make sure Principal Myers ain't coming along. Good-God-a'*mighty,* what a hard-ass. I mean, I appreciate him giving me this opportunity and all, but he would have a fuckin' conniption, you know what I'm saying?

Anyway, uh, help me clear this desk off. Yeah, you two.

Just—I don't know—pile all that shit over in the corner. Good. All right, somebody hit the lights.

Now, y'all know "Macho Man," right? What about "Y.M.C.A."? All right, I usually start off with one or the other of them. Either way, chicks dig it—*oops*, sorry, Deb. Anyway, let's go for "Y.M.C.A." Y'all can sing it, right? Let's hear it! Yeah, like that. You got it. Sounds good. You too, man. *Yeah!* Cool. Keep on going like that.

Okay now, the first thing I do is strut on out into the room. I got my hands on my hips, got my head a'bobbin' up and down, I'm taking a good long look around. All them chicks is giggling and trying not to look at me—although some of them is starin' straight at me, you know what I mean? And that's when I do a little jerk, like . . . *this.* That gets them going pretty damn good. They're starting to loosen up a little, okay? And serious now, that's the whole point of this. I'm a paid professional here doing a real job. No foolin' around. This ain't high school no more, you hear me? Anyway, next, I do a little twirl, like, uh . . . *this.* All right? They're all gettin' into it now.

And then, next, just when they're thinking that might be everything ol' Wags has got—buh-*lam*—I go straight for what I call the Humper Pumper. First, I take off my shirt like this. Uh, *damn*, if I can just . . . Hey, can one of y'all help me pull my arm out here? Okay, thanks. So, I take off my shirt and then I lasso it in the air over my head like this. Then I toss it to one of the ladies—or sometimes I just throw it right down on the floor, okay? Except, uh, I don't wanna get my shirt all dirty and shit here at school, you know? Can you hold on to this for me? Thanks now.

Okay, anyway, then I *pump* it, all right? This is the part that gets them chicks a'squealin'. I say, "Pump it!" You see what I'm doin' here? "Hump it!" That's right, yeah!

All right, y'all try it. C'mon, get your asses *up*. I did my thing, now let's see what you got. Kev, Deb, everybody— let's go! Everyone get in line. That's it, start back there in the back and just come on up. Keep on singin'! That's right. Now, you—yeah, I'm talking to *you:* "Pump it, pump it, pump it good." That's it, girl! Don't be afraid. Now you get up behind her, Kev. Yeah, like that, man. "Hump it like you know you should." All right! Now the rest of y'all swing the line around this way. That's it! Keep on goin'!

Okay, Debbie, your turn. Pump it, girl. Hey, what are you doin'? I didn't say "chick"! Where you goin'? Wait, don't slam that door! *Shit!*

Okay, everyone, that's it. Turn them lights on. Let's get this all cleaned up. Quick! Old Myers is gonna be down here in about half a frickin' second. Yeah, just put everything back on the desk. It don't have to be straight. Everybody back in your seats. *Now,* you hear?

All right, that's cool, that's cool. Everybody simmer down for a second, okay? Wow, that was . . . fucked up, you know? Whoa! What the hell was I thinkin' letting you talk me into that? Oh, well, it's my own damn fault. And serious now, you know what? I don't give a shit. Y'all done good, all right? I mean it. Myers coulda walked in here any time, but you didn't let that stop you. You *went* for it—

and that's exactly what I been on about! I know this might be . . . *Damn,* I can't believe I'm gettin' choked up about this. *Shit!* Where'd that come from? I need something to wipe my eyes with. Oh yeah, uh, I need my shirt back. Thanks.

But serious now, I come in here expectin' to give y'all a little advice, tell y'all about the big, bad world out there, but you know what? Y'all are gonna be okay. That ain't no bullshit. And you know what? If any of y'all *do* wanna go for Girls Nite, you just tell Miss Pincus I sent you, because that was some of the most amazin' Humper-Pumpering I have *ever* seen. I shit you not.

Anyway, *damn,* y'all make me proud. *Wow.* I guess, though, we gotta get on back to them problems and what-not y'all gotta do. Yeah, I know, I know . . . bummer. But we're probably gonna be in trouble in a few minutes. Let's all simmer down now, okay? Simmer down. Just act cool, like nothin' happened. All right?

So, uh, back to where we was . . . Anybody got any questions or anything for ol' Wags? Anybody? All right then, I'll just sit up here. No problem.

But hey, serious now, not to interrupt or anything, but speaking of giving y'all a little advice, I probably should tell you—before Myers gets here—what to do if the cops ever come a'bangin' on your door in the middle of the night. Lesson one? Grab your stash and start flushin'. You hear what I'm sayin'?

On Top of It All

GWEN AND VALERIE AT LARGE

1982

I was, like, washing down my last bite of toast with my last gulp of juice when the doorbell rang and I heard my mother talking a mile a minute in that cartoony voice she always uses with my friends—that high-pitched, country-sounding stream of "Can you be-*lieve* this?" and "Why, I simply can-*not* get over that." And then I could hear Valerie going, "Yes ma'am" and "That's right," sounding all happy and like she actually cared. But this was the third day in a row I'd made her wait, and I knew she was pissed off at me.

She came around the corner into the kitchen, Mom—to my complete mortification—shuffling along behind her in the Garfield-the-Cat bedroom slippers Dad gave her for Christmas and still chattering away: "Gwen, darlin', Valerie's here, did you have enough to eat? You better hurry up 'n' get ready."

"I *know*, Mom," I said, squinching up my face real good.

Yes, I was being a queen bitch, but I swear to God, she thinks I'm still, like, thirteen.

Val was pushing her fists way deep down into the pockets of her pink zip-up sweatshirt, and her face was just a blank, no expression whatsoever. Except then she sort of flared her nostrils like she'd caught a gross, disgusting whiff of something or other, and she leaned in close to me and whispered, "Yeah, get *ready,* we gotta *go.*" Maybe it was her own breath she was smelling, because it stunk like an ashtray, and here it was barely eight-thirty.

I hurried up the kitchen stairs, with Mom going on and on about how crazy it is in the morning trying to get the kids out of the house, and how they just don't wanna get out of bed, and oh, by the way, did you know it's supposed to storm later this week? And I could've just about died picturing Valerie—ready to kill me—nodding and smiling and tapping her foot and saying, "Yes ma'am, uh huh, I know what you mean."

I peed, brushed my teeth and hair, and checked my makeup in the bathroom. Then I went and stood in front of the full-length mirror in my parents' room, smoothing out my peach-colored top and the hip-hugger jeans that Jeff loved so much, always telling me how cute and perky my ass looked in them. Even so, I absolutely could not decide if I looked okay. But it was way too late to change, so I called down that I was heading out the front door. I didn't need to listen to any more of Mom's yakking, and I definitely did *not* want to hear her nagging me about how much mascara and blush I had on, like she always does.

Outside, Val and I hopped into her buttercup-yellow Beetle she'd kept running in front of the house. When I glanced over, there was Mom waving at us through the bay window in our living room—but I pretended I didn't see her as Valerie put the car in gear and it lurched forward, pinning us back against our seats.

As she turned onto Lee-Jackson Avenue, Valerie was like, "Dammit, Gwen, this is bullshit with you and your mom every morning."

I ignored her. What was I supposed to say? That it was Mom's fault for letting me sleep till eight o'clock? Valerie would've snorted and lectured me on being self-reliant (she loves using that word) and how she and her mom have, like, an "understanding"—how her mom treats her like a grownup, and while that sounds cool and all, it's really about responsibility.

"Yeah, I can stay out as late as I want, and she's not allowed in my room," Valerie told me once. "But then on the other hand, she's not gonna bail me out if I get busted or sweet-talk the principal if I fuck up at school, like your parents would. It's all on me."

At the time, I didn't point out that Valerie *was* fucking up at school (while I was doing okay with B's and C's). Or that maybe her mom had better things to do than worry about Valerie and her problems. I mean, why push it? Val's okay, even if she gets on her high horse sometimes. Besides, it's fun cruising around with her and doing crazy stuff together. I don't mean sticking up the 7-Eleven or anything like that, just run-of-the-mill pot smoking and beer drinking and making out with Jeff and Tony over at the rock quarry or up at the top of Mount Warren.

Anyway, Valerie and I were about halfway to school when I *did* think of something to say. Looking back on it, I admit that part of it was to impress her. But the other part was that I really, truly did not want to deal with school that day, so I was like, "Hey, you wanna skip?"

"Are you *serious*?" Valerie's tone was that sort of mock-shock she's so good at, like I'd said, "Hey, you wanna go kill somebody?" But then she slowed down and pulled the car over. We were in the middle of the deserted campus of the old Brookford Military Academy—BMA—that we drive through sometimes as a shortcut.

We sat there for a minute, the Beetle puttering away like a lawnmower, Valerie smoking a cigarette, both of us peering out at all the boarded-up, cinder-block buildings. When I was five or six—before the school went, like, bankrupt and shut down—my dad would sometimes take me over to watch the graduation ceremonies in the spring. He'd stand on the grassy slope above the parade grounds, me perched on his shoulders, while the cadets marched and saluted and went through their formations, all of them dressed in their official maroon shirts and black pants with the wide gold stripes down the sides. At the end of the ceremonies, they'd toss their caps into the air. I remember Daddy picking one off the ground once—an officer's-type hat with a shiny bill—and plunking it on my head. It was way too big for me, though, and fell down over my ears and eyes, and I started bawling. (I probably wasn't too psyched about all the super-loud guns and cannons they kept firing, either.) But suddenly there were a dozen cadets around us. I'll never forget that feeling, being on top of the world with all those fresh-faced boys in their beautiful uniforms, all grinning and joking and trying to make me feel better.

Valerie was squinting and blowing smoke out one side of her mouth. She was like, "You got any tests today?"

We only skip school on days when we don't have any tests or labs or anything we get graded on. (We can't worry about pop quizzes because they're going to happen whether we like it or not.) The next day we tell Mrs. Howdyshell in the office and all our teachers that we forgot our note from our parents. They're like, "Okay, but bring it in tomorrow"—but then when tomorrow comes, they've forgotten all about it.

The problem is you can't do it too much or they'll catch on. This year, we'd only skipped once before, back in October, so I figured it was about time again.

I went through my classes in my head. PE and art, no problem. Geometry, clear. Biology, clear. English, maybe a pop quiz on *The Crucible,* but no biggie. French, are you kidding? Mrs. Hauser hates giving tests. She's so shitty at French herself, I don't think she even understands our answers. *Definitely* clear!

I was like, "I'm cool. What about you?"

"I'm always cool," said Valerie. "Tony gave me two joints I've been dying to smoke. Let's get high and raise some hell."

She put the car in gear and we took off, both of us screaming "Woooo!" and rolling our windows all the way down and letting the wind blow our hair everywhere. Valerie did a U-ey and got back on Lee-Jackson and we sped out of town.

We jumped on the interstate for a few miles before taking the Wells Corner exit and driving out into the country, the mountains blue and crystally clear on the horizon. Valerie had Tony's AC/DC tape with her, and we sang along with "Highway to Hell" at the top of our lungs for about a minute. But then we spotted a sheriff's car coming our way, bobbing over the hill ahead of us, so Valerie switched the music off and slowed down. He flew by going the other direction. Even if he'd noticed us, he probably would've had more important things to do than play truant officer. But since Valerie had those joints with her, we were both feeling a little bit paranoid, and we rode along in silence until we reached the 909 turnoff.

Route 909 is this gravel road that runs for about half a mile beside some manure-smelling cow pastures and a wide, shallow creek. It also takes you to the base of Mount Warren, this real big hill—or small mountain or whatever—that's on the edge of town and where a lot of us high-school kids go to party. At the top, there are a couple of picnic tables that look like they've been there forever, but if you walk through the woods, you come out to this amazing view. You can see all of Brookford from up there—downtown, the busy parts of Winchester Boulevard and Lee-Jackson, everything. Plus the old historic neighborhoods on the far side of the train overpass. In the other direction, you can see most of Turnersburg, pushed right up against the mountains.

Anytime we drive up there—whether it's just a few of us or a big party—I always stare and stare at the view until I remember everything I'm seeing. Then I try to paint or draw the scene at home, getting the colors right for whatever season or time of day it is. I've done it about twenty times, and all my scenes are different, even though it's really the same scene. Art class at school is, like, a joke, but since I do art on my own, the teacher is usually cool with me doing whatever I want.

Anyway, with Valerie that day, instead of heading up Mount Warren, we decided to stay on 909. It's completely hidden from the main road, and we've never had a problem with anyone driving by or hassling us when we were partying.

Val stopped the car on this bank that juts out above the creek. She reached for her purse in the back seat and dug through it until she found one of the joints. I watched out my side mirror, keeping my eyes peeled just in case anybody *did* come driving along the road, as she flicked her lighter and took a big hit off the joint, then passed it to me.

It was fairly good weed. Almost right away I could feel a nice pressure behind my eyes, and my tongue went kind of numb like it always does. We took our time, toking slow and easy, giggling and forgetting to check for cars, then remembering and getting real serious for a second, then giggling and smoking some more when we saw that no one was coming.

When the joint was done, Valerie stubbed it out in the ashtray and dropped the roach into a plastic baggie she had in her purse. Then we listened to the AC/DC tape for a while. I was pretty stoned and for a long time just stared straight out the windshield at the green and yellow fields stretching away into the distance and the dogwood trees starting to bloom like crazy on the other side of the creek, smiling at all the intense color and how gorgeous it all looked—especially with the sun breaking over Mount Warren behind us and lighting everything up. I was also thinking about Jeff, how he'd finally, *finally* said "I love you" the last time we were out there and how amazing it was going to feel when I decided to let him make love to me. My stomach got all warm and tingly, like it does when I take a big swig from a bottle of Boone's Farm.

Valerie, though, was definitely not in the same place as me because all of a sudden she was like, "Tony is such a fucking asshole sometimes." Of course, like I always do, I had to say Why. And of course she started in on how all he ever wants to do is get in her pants—and while she enjoys sex with him and all, she wants him to love her for *her*, not because she'll fuck him. She got all teary and lit a cigarette and looked out her window, and I didn't know what to say at that point. Then she kind of sniffled and started the car. "Let's get outta here," she said. "I'm hungry."

Well, it was then that it finally dawned on us that we hadn't checked to see if we had any money between us. We were so excited to skip school and smoke. Now we did check. I only had some pennies and a nickel or two in my purse. Valerie was flat broke.

She was like, "We are so stupid! What the hell are we

gonna do? My mouth's a ball of cotton, and I'm getting the munchies. And what about lunch?" Then she glanced at her gas gauge. "And what about gas? Fuck!"

I laughed—I couldn't help it—but Val was on a tear. "I can't fucking believe this!" she kept saying. She turned the car around and floored it back to the main road, then drove super fast back toward the interstate. At the last second, she turned onto this other road that winds its way toward Lake Pamunkey and into Turnersburg eventually. After a couple of miles, she pulled into a Shell filling station that's there in the middle of, like, nowhere. Easing up next to the pump, she was like, "Stay in the car." She grabbed her purse and went inside.

I saw her through the plate-glass window of the small white building, talking to the man behind the counter. He was wearing a funny little cap and this ugly brown jumpsuit. Valerie was flashing her teeth and pointing at the car. She was flipping her long hair away from the side of her face and over her shoulder. The man got off his stool, opened the door behind him, and went into the garage. He looked about a hundred years old and moved so slow he could've been stoned himself. Valerie disappeared too, but I couldn't see where she went. Then, after a minute, the man came back through the door and set something on the counter. And suddenly there was Valerie again, hands on her hips and chatting with the guy, nodding up and down like they were long-lost cousins or something.

She walked out to the car and plopped her purse down on the floor behind the driver's seat. "Don't say a word," she said. Then she started pumping gas. When she finished, she sort of crept around to her side, like, real slow before jumping in the seat and tearing out of the lot and onto the road again. I looked over my shoulder. That old guy was waddling out near the pump and shaking his fist and yelling at us. But with his old-man eyes, there was no way he was going to make out our license plate number from way back there.

"Oh my God-oh my God!" Valerie was saying, laughing real hard before coughing this horrible dry cough that sounded like she was gonna croak.

I wanted to hear what happened, but I waited as she coughed and tried to catch her breath and at the same time drove us all over those country roads trying to get us back to the interstate without having to go by the filling station again.

"Get my pocketbook," she said at last. When I did, I saw that she'd stuffed a bottle of Mountain Dew and two packs of Cheese-its and a Twinkie and a Hershey bar inside. I started laughing so hard I almost dropped the soda as I handed it to her.

Valerie drove us back to BMA, gulping from the Mountain Dew every few minutes or so. She steered down this narrow, concrete alley that runs between two of the buildings and overlooks the old football field. Her eyes were red and glassy. Her cheeks were all flushed from laughing and coughing. She took another big guzzle from the bottle before telling me what she'd said to the guy at the Shell station.

"I needed to ask for something he'd have to go into the

garage for," she said. "It couldn't be oil or windshield wipers 'cause he had those right behind the counter." She stared down the alley for a second, her jaw kind of like dropping open—I was getting spacey myself—and then she handed me the bottle. "I remembered Tony telling me I needed to replace my fan belt soon. He said he could do it for me if I bought the belt. So I just told that old guy I needed a fan belt for my '73 Beetle. When he brought it out, I said, 'Good, just hold it while I fill the tank, then I'll pay for everything at once.'"

My head was all droopy by now, but listening to her made me feel like we were in a James Bond movie or something. I was like, "Wow, good thinking."

She tapped the side of her head with her index finger. "It's what I've been saying, Gwen. You gotta be on top of it all."

We were both starting to come down, and we got quiet, finishing off the munchies and the soda. I got kind of a lonely feeling being cooped up in that tiny car and surrounded by all those old buildings that were making me think of a prison or a penitentiary or something like that. After a while I was like, "Let's get out and look around."

We went to the very end of the alley—up to the dented metal guardrail that keeps you from falling straight down this rocky cliff onto the football field—and looked across the way to Lee-Jackson. There were no cars driving by. That made me feel even lonelier. Plus, the sky was clouding up, getting all white and smeary-looking. I was missing that nice warm sunshine we'd had out on Route 909.

Pretty soon we noticed that the heavy gray door at the back of one of the bigger buildings was standing part way open. Valerie wandered over, taking the paved pathway leading right up to it. She peeked in and then called me over, saying, "Oh my *God,* you have *got* to see this!"

I followed her inside. It was this huge, ancient room where the school's old swim team must've practiced and had their meets and stuff. The big pool was drained, but I swear the place still smelled like chlorine and mildew. Built-in bleachers ran next to it, and there were a bunch of open shower stalls at one end. The walls had to be at least thirty feet high, covered floor to ceiling with all these little maroon and gold tiles, even though there were lots of chalky patches where tiles had fallen off. It was cool to see those same school colors the cadets had worn when they'd marched on the parade grounds all those years ago.

Val slid over the edge and onto the dirty, cobwebby floor of the dry pool, at the shallow end. "This is wild," she said, her voice echoing everywhere. "Come on in, the water's perfect." She laughed at her little joke as I climbed down the rickety ladder into the pool too. When I turned to face her, she was lighting up that second joint. At first, I was a little paranoid, wondering whether some old janitor might come shuffling in and bust us. But I didn't think that was likely, so we sat down—which was really weird, kind of imagining we were underwater—and passed the joint back and forth, gazing up at the walls and the cracked glass of the dirty skylight windows in the ceiling way up above us.

Once we'd burned the joint down to nothing, Valerie was like, "Watch this" and she licked the lit end of the roach, sort of, like, dousing the red coal in her spit. Then she popped the whole thing into her mouth and swallowed it, which made me feel pretty nauseous. "Tony showed me," she said and grinned. But then she got that look on her face again and I knew she was thinking about Tony and him being a jerk and all.

Maybe I was just stoned and feeling a little sappy, I don't know, but I felt bad for her all of a sudden. I didn't make a big deal of it or anything, but I put my hand on top of hers and squeezed a little bit. I was surprised when she squeezed back and then leaned her head against my shoulder. And then we just sat there for a good long while without talking.

Finally, though, she sat up straight and wiped her eyes, and we dusted ourselves off and climbed out of the pool. We went back to the guardrail outside, Valerie chain-smoking and me just spacing on everything. Someone had spray-painted on the rail—like, years ago—"BMA Rules!" Later, somebody else had crossed through "Rules!" with red paint and written "Sucks My BM!" And since the school had gone defunct, no one had ever come back to take up for BMA again, which *I* thought really sucked. I kind of laughed about it, though, but before I could tell Valerie what I was thinking, she brought up food again, and I realized I was hungry too. We weren't too psyched to try swiping any more munchies, so Valerie suggested we sneak over to her house.

"My mom had some meetings this morning and won't be

there," she said. "And even if she does show up, we'll just say we decided to come home for lunch. She won't give two shits about that."

"But it's early," I said.

Valerie was like, "She won't notice, okay?"

Well, I was thinking she probably *would* notice. And besides that, I was *not* thrilled about having to drive down our street for everyone to see. Technically, we're not supposed to leave school grounds for lunch anyway, even though a lot of kids sneak off to McDonald's and Three Brothers Pizza. My parents, though, would have a cow if they caught me doing it.

But Valerie said we'd just leave her car at BMA and walk home through the woods between Lee-Jackson and our neighborhood. My parents were at work too, so they wouldn't see us. And if any of the neighbors asked — "Which they *won't*," Valerie said — we'd give them the same excuse about leaving school to eat lunch at home.

I still wasn't convinced this was a good idea, but I decided to go along with it. My stomach was rumbling and I didn't have a better plan. So we cut across the BMA campus toward our street, keeping close to the buildings and away from the road. When we finally got to Lee-Jackson, we darted across the road and into the woods, following the trail that comes out next to Mrs. Edwards' little brick house, two doors down from Valerie's. I was feeling really paranoid now and just marched forward along the sidewalk, looking straight ahead, ready to pretend I didn't see them if any neighbors popped up. But they didn't, and soon we'd reached Valerie's. She took the house key from under a potted plant on the front porch, and then we were safely inside.

Valerie's house is like a museum or something. Her mother keeps all these antiques on display in their living room and den. A grandfather clock, carved wooden armchairs with super high backs, porcelain vases and lamps, beautiful portraits and paintings. It's so spotless and straightened up, you're afraid to sit anywhere. And the whole place smells like lemon Pledge. But then you go upstairs into Valerie's room, and she's got clothes thrown on the floor and ashtrays overflowing with butts and half-drunk glasses of Coke on her desk and her bedside table. I'm one to talk, I guess, but it's amazing that Val's mom lets her live like this. My parents are always on my case about cleaning up my stuff.

Anyway, we went up to her room, and Valerie flipped her stereo on and lit a cigarette. I sat down on the edge of her bed. She started rifling through all the crap in her drawers and scanning the shelves of her closet, until at last she was like, "A-*ha*!" and held up a baggie that had maybe a half joint's worth of weed in it. "I *knew* I put this somewhere," she said, tossing the baggie onto the top of her desk and rifling some more until she found this cute little purple pipe I'd never seen before.

I wasn't sure I wanted to smoke any more, and I was about to mention that we should head to the kitchen for something to eat—which was, like, the whole reason we were there in the first place. But Val had already filled the small bowl and lit it and was passing it to me. So I took a long toke, handed the pipe back, and went over to the window, trying to hold the smoke in my lungs as long as I could. Below me, in front of the house, Valerie's mom had just pulled up in her nice Toyota and was swinging the door open and stepping out onto the sidewalk.

I went on, like, automatic pilot. I blew my smoke out in a big blue cloud, took the pipe from Valerie, and jammed it into my pocket with my thumb over the bowl. "Your mom's home," I said.

We completely forgot our excuse of skipping lunch. Valerie was like, "Get in the closet." She lay down next to her bed and shimmied on her back across the carpet, squeezing under the low bed frame.

I could hear the front-door lock clicking open as I stepped around Valerie's pink beanbag chair, got in the closet, and pulled the door shut. I felt so stoned then—and my heart was beating so fast—that it was all I could do to stand up straight in that dark, musty closet without keeling over. Plus, I suddenly had to pee really bad.

The front door closed and immediately Valerie's mom called out, "Valerie? Hello?" which really got my heart thumping. I still wasn't remembering our excuse, and I guess I was mainly afraid of getting caught smoking pot. I was sure the room reeked like hell.

Valerie's mother came straight upstairs—I heard each step creaking—then walked right into the room, not hesitating at all. "Valerie," she said again, this time more like a statement of fact than a question. It sounded to me like she was on the other side of the room, but then the closet's doorknob turned and the door swung open, and there was Valerie's mom looking at me like I had seven heads. She was like, "Where's Valerie?"

I glanced toward the bed—I couldn't help it—but she kept her eyes on me. "What the hell are you doing here?"

Valerie's mom has always been real nice to me, but she was pissed off now. It hit me that she thought I was alone, that I had broken into her house or something.

"Where is *Valerie*?" she practically yelled.

I was about ready to bust out crying, but then Valerie called out from under the bed, "I'm *here*, o-*kay*?"

We watched as Valerie slid out from under the bed, and the look of utter astonishment on her mom's face made me want to curl up and die.

"What are y'all doing here?" she asked, her face suddenly all pale and pasty-looking. I guess we'd given her a good scare. She must've been flipping out, wondering whether there were burglars in the house when she walked through the door.

"We skipped school, all *right*?" Valerie said in that obnoxious voice she uses sometimes, like you're a complete idiot.

Valerie's mom stood kind of, like, shaking in her pantsuit for a second, then stomped out of the room. I looked at Valerie just as her mother shouted from down the hall, "I want you girls out of here *now*!"

I headed straight for the front door. It was only when I got outside that I realized Valerie was right behind me. She hadn't stopped to say anything else to her mom.

We cut through the woods and across the BMA campus without talking, and I squatted behind the car and peed. Then the two of us just drove around the rest of the day—up to the Turnersburg mall, then back to Route 909, and finally over to the rock quarry for an hour or so. We tried to laugh about what had happened, and Valerie kept assuring me that her mother wouldn't tell my parents. But I had a real bad feeling in my stomach and didn't look forward to going home.

By three o'clock, I was totally burned out and starving. Valerie dropped me off in front of my house and was like, "Good luck." Then she was gone, her yellow Beetle puttering away down the street.

My mother was waiting for me in the front hallway. As soon as I walked through the door, she laid into me with "What were you *thinking*, skipping *school*?" and "Valerie's mother told me *all* about it" and "Hiding in her *closet*?" and on and on and on. And then more from my father when he got home.

The good news is they didn't find out about the pot smoking. Valerie's mom only mentioned smelling cigarette smoke to my mother. That's what tipped her off that someone was in the house. My parents know Valerie smokes, so they didn't grill me about that, thank God. The bad news is I got grounded, which was a bummer.

And the worse news is that Jeff broke up with me the

next day. I was sitting in the cafeteria when he came over and said he needed to talk to me outside. There we were, standing on the hill in front of the school, and he was like, "I just don't think it's gonna work out."

But you know what I said? "I don't think so either." He made a face like I'd punched him in the stomach, which is what I should have done. Then I went and sat under the two ivy-covered trees at the bottom of the hill and cried my stupid eyes out.

Later, I saw Valerie in the hall between classes and told her about Jeff. She grinned and told me she'd broken up with Tony earlier in the day. I started crying again, not just because I was sad—which I was—but because it seemed so perfect for a minute, the two of us there together, like we'd sort of accomplished something. Which I guess we had.

Bully

Fresh from the shower and a scrub with his spearmint-kiwi body wash, Mitchell Taylor stands in front of the kitchen bulletin board with a green bath sheet around his waist like a hula skirt. He sips from his tumbler of blueberry pomegranate juice and scans the collection of tacked-up papers. Fliers, printouts, calendars, red and yellow notices from Henry's school. How does Gwen prioritize any of this clutter?

The corner of a Visa bill peeks out from behind a chocolate-sauce recipe that her best friend, Valerie, gave her. Mitchell starts to move the recipe to another spot on the board but then reminds himself that this is Gwen's domain. Ever since the night he tried to organize the spare bedroom she uses for her home business designing custom greeting cards, she has insisted that he not interfere with her house-management system, as she calls it. She did suggest that he could wash a pot or pan or at least run the dishwasher occasionally. But he's happy to consider the after-dinner cleaning part of her system too, especially since the dirty kitchenware makes him anxious.

A few soiled plates and saucers, though, are nothing compared to the chaos of this bulletin board. Mitchell closes his eyes and pictures his desk at work. The polished blond wood, the neat stacks of files and folders, how his computer, rolodex, and telephone form a satisfying pattern of right angles. He takes a deep breath through his nose and exhales slowly, as his yoga-class instructor has taught him to do.

When he opens his eyes, he notices Henry's class picture at the bottom of the large board, pinched between the wooden frame and the cork backing. He hasn't taken a good look at the photo since Gwen displayed it there months earlier, and he leans over to study it. All of the third-graders, along with their teacher, Ms. Funk, glance slightly to one side, straining to hold their smiles in place, as if the photographer had called "Cheese" too soon, before he'd finished fiddling with his camera.

Mitchell locates Henry sitting cross-legged on the floor with the other small boys in the class. Behind them is a row of girls in folding chairs. And standing behind the chairs, looming over the rest of the group, are the big kids—six or seven boys and girls with that look of self-satisfaction that all big kids seem to have.

"Cretins," Mitchell says.

Gwen comes into the kitchen in her flannel tartan robe.

"Morning. When's your appointment?" She runs water into the coffee pot.

"Gwen, which one of these endomorphs has been picking on Henry?" Mitchell says, examining each face.

"*Endomorphs*? My *gosh*, Mitch. Craig Hightower is the little boy who's been acting out."

Mitchell taps the photo. "This one, am I right?" He rests the tip of his finger on the chest of a tall kid with broad shoulders and a particularly obnoxious-looking smirk on his face.

Gwen sighs, flips on the coffee machine, and walks over next to Mitchell. "No, that's him." She points to a slight-framed, curly-headed boy sitting on the floor near Henry.

"That scrawny runt is the bully?"

"He's not a bully. He's rambunctious and plays a little rough sometimes."

"Like when he pushed Henry down on the playground."

Gwen puts on her best I'm-trying-incredibly-hard-to-be-patient smile. "It wasn't that cut and dried. And as I told you, Craig's mother *and* Ms. Funk *and* Mr. Blackstone are aware of his behavior." She goes back to the counter, takes down a few cups and bowls from the cabinets above it, and scans the boxes of breakfast cereals crammed together on two of the shelves.

Mitchell sets his empty juice glass on the table and comes up behind her. "Okay, it's taken care of. I just don't want Henry getting hurt. Our precious Henry, right?"

Gwen doesn't turn around, but Mitchell is certain he's

made her smile. He feels her shoulders relax as he massages them. He strokes her long, soft hair, moving it to one side to kiss the back of her neck. "Hey," he says, pressing against her, "what say I whip off my towel?"

"Mitch, our precious Henry is *up*." Gwen shrugs his hands away but turns and kisses his cheek. "Why don't you get dressed? Don't you have to be at Doctor B's soon?"

"Not until ten thirty," Mitchell says.

"I assume you're not going into the office afterwards?"

"You assume right. You know I hate half days. I'll work from home this afternoon. That's what my cell phone and laptop are for."

"Well, maybe we can have a date *then*," she says, and kisses him once more.

Mitchell cinches his towel and grins. "We'll see," he says. Then he heads up the back stairs, taking them one at a time and counting them off to himself in a whisper.

On the landing outside the upstairs bathroom, he encounters Henry, dressed in the *SpongeBob* pajamas he inherited from one of his older cousins.

"Well, hello," Mitchell says. "Mornin', Tiger."

Henry sucks in his cheeks and tries not to laugh at this ongoing joke he shares with his father. His face is waffle-ironed with sheet marks. A wide ridge of his thick, sandy hair sticks straight out on one side of his head.

"Champ? Little man?" Mitchell says.

Henry stamps his foot in mock protest. "Daddy!"

"Tiger-champ-man? Wait—Tigerman! *There* you go."

"You are so weird," Henry says, turning toward the stairs.

"Hold on," Mitchell says. "First of all, Tigerman would be *extremely* cool, you have to admit."

"Maybe."

"And secondly"—Mitchell lowers his voice—"how's everything at school?"

Henry eyes his father suspiciously. "Uh, okay."

"Listen, I know it's no fun when kids are mean. But any time someone is mean to you, like Craig, you need to tell the teacher. He's not allowed to act that way."

"Craig's all right," says Henry, looking distracted and impatient.

"Well, my point is, there are *rules*, Tigerman. Okay?" He gives Henry what he hopes is an important-looking nod.

"Henry, come eat your breakfast," Gwen calls from the kitchen.

Henry starts down the stairs.

"Okay?" Mitchell says after him.

"Okay, I *heard* you!" Henry says without a backward glance.

‡‡‡

Mitchell sees his internist every two months, insisting each time on full blood work, urinalysis, and pulmonary and cardiological screening. His doctor, Zack Bloomgarden—"Dr. B" as everyone loves calling him—has told Mitchell that testing this often is not the most effective use of his time and money. But Mitchell is convinced that his routine is the best way to prevent the innumerable cancers, syndromes, and disorders that could be lurking in his body's seemingly healthy cells, ready to strike without warning. Besides, he enjoys the feeling of accomplishment he gets after every appointment.

The western edge of the county where he and Gwen live—ten miles outside of Brookford—is semi-rural horse country. As he tools along Route 219 in his spotless white Volvo, he passes the converted farmhouses, mansions and McMansions, and older traditional estate houses that sit back from the road on five- and ten-acre spreads. For Mitchell, the elegance of these luxury homes is outdone only by the precision with which the lines of the properties are drawn: slate walks neatly dividing front lawns from ruler-straight rows of daffodils and hyacinth; short stone walls and rough-cut cedar fences cleanly separating backyards from open pasture and imposing stands of oak, beech, and pine.

It's mid April, still cool out, and Mitchell adjusts the front windows up and down until both are cracked open an even inch. He tunes the radio to the classical station out of Turnersburg. The announcer is welcoming listeners to the annual Mozart Marathon. Mitchell shakes his head as the first movement of *Eine kleine Nachtmusik* begins playing. Such a pedestrian choice, he thinks. But then he settles in, admitting to himself how much he enjoys the piece. It reminds him not only of his college days—when he, the computer geek, and Gwen, the commercial art major, first met and fell in love—but also of his and Gwen's first years in Brookford. She grew up in the small Southern town and had no trouble convincing Mitchell that it was where they should start their family together. He loved the area's forests and the long sweep of its valleys, the crisp, clean air, the ancient mountains painting the horizon blue in every direction.

Whistling quietly now, Mitchell cruises over the road's small hills and around its gentle turns, taking comfort in the familiar surroundings and beautiful vistas, but careful to observe the speed limit of 40. Most people drive much faster. On some mornings, in fact, he has found himself at the front of a long, snaking line of cars all bearing down on him from behind. In response, he usually turns up the radio and does his yogic breathing exercises. He doesn't like being pressured into going faster than he's supposed to. At this time of day, though—two hours after the rush of commuter traffic through Brookford and onto the interstate toward Turnersburg—Mitchell has the road virtually to himself. Except for a FedEx delivery van and a green BMW going in the opposite direction, he hasn't spotted any vehicles since leaving home.

The dashboard clock blinks to 10:15 just as Mitchell reaches the halfway point, the four-way intersection ten minutes from Dr. Bloomgarden's office. Perfect, he thinks. Time enough to finish his drive and still be strolling through the door five minutes early.

After the intersection, as he's speeding up again, a cherry red SUV barrels out from a side road directly into his path. Mitchell jams on the brakes and blasts the horn. An oversize suburban tank—driven, no doubt, by a soccer mom gabbing away on her phone, oblivious to everything around her—it careens down the road in front of Mitchell and around the next bend. Without thinking, Mitchell presses on the accelerator. He zooms along the road and around the turn as well. The SUV is already flying over the hill a hundred yards ahead. Mitchell presses even harder on the gas, but then eases off the pedal. He taps the brakes, checking his mirror to make sure no one is behind him. His pulse drums in his ears, but he laughs at how his emotions almost got the better of him. What was he planning to do if he'd actually caught up with the other driver? Haul her out of the car and lecture her on the importance of sharing the road? He takes in a lungful of air, checks his speedometer, and proceeds, glad to have the road to himself again. As a gorgeously blossoming Mount Warren comes into view, he turns the radio up a notch. He puts both hands on the steering wheel and pushes himself back into the comfort of his plush seat.

Enjoying his drive again, he soon reaches his favorite stretch, the long straightaway where thick woods crowd the road on either side. The trees' branches form a canopy overhead, filtering the sunlight in such a way that everything is bathed in a cool shade of green, creating a sense that one is steering through the depths of an unspoiled, undiscovered sea.

At the far end of the tunnel, he's awakened from his daydream when he notices brake lights ahead. As he approaches, he sees that the car is the red SUV from before, stopped at an angle in the right lane. Telling himself to stay calm, he turns on his blinker, ready to pass. As he pulls into the left lane, the SUV takes off. Mitchell swerves back into his lane, trailing behind the other car. A temporary license tag is posted low inside its back windshield, but he can't make out the numbers; a "Party Naked!" bumper sticker on the outside covers them. Within half a mile, the SUV slows from 35 to 30 and then down to 20. Mitchell moves into the left lane again and coasts alongside the other car. Glancing over, he sees not a housewife but two teenage boys in the front seats laughing hysterically.

"Ha, ha, big joke," Mitchell says. They tear away again.

Mitchell speeds up too and follows them to the end of Route 219, where the road narrows to a one-lane train underpass a couple of blocks outside Brookford's downtown area. Halfway through the brick-and-concrete archway, the SUV skids to a halt. Mitchell hits the brakes, sending his briefcase off the passenger seat and onto the floor. "Dammit!" he shouts.

The SUV is parked in the center of the unmarked road, leaving no room for Mitchell to squeeze by on either side. He realizes too late that he should have taken the turn two miles back that would have brought him into town from the south, along Winchester Boulevard and through Brookford's main underpass. But he was too caught up in following the SUV. He could turn around, but it's already 10:23. His stomach rumbles at the thought of running late, and he blows his horn. The boys—young men, really, one with a close-shaved head, the other sporting a black goatee—sit sideways in their seats, grinning and watching Mitchell through the back windshield. They make no move to face forward and continue driving.

Mitchell wants to avoid a confrontation, but the minutes

are ticking by. He opens his door and steps out of the car. The SUV pulls away, and he jumps behind the wheel again. As he's yanking his seatbelt on, the SUV backs up to where it was before, trapping him once more. He leans on the horn. "Get the hell out of here!"

The teenagers are laughing and high-fiving. Mitchell checks behind him, then peers up the road toward Dr. Bloomgarden's office building. He can see light traffic flowing along Brookford's main thoroughfare, but no one—not one car—is heading in their direction. It's 10:27; he won't be on time for his appointment now even if the boys drive away immediately. Keeping an eye on the SUV, he reaches over to grab his cell phone out of the briefcase on the floor. He strains against the seatbelt's shoulder strap, rummages through his papers with his fingertips, and at last fishes it out. As he's sitting up again, a horn blasts behind him. The SUV rumbles forward, makes a quick right turn, and disappears down the street. Mitchell looks in the rearview mirror, sees a dark car, and waves his hand to thank the driver.

Afraid it's past ten thirty, he avoids looking at the clock. His shirt feels damp against his skin, and a hint of body odor has started to mingle with the fresh scent from his shower. He drives ahead slowly, glancing between the road and the phone. He punches the familiar contact number on his speed dial and puts the phone to his ear. As he waits for an answer, there's another blast behind him, like a fire-engine horn. He checks the rearview again. The dark car is an unmarked police cruiser. Its front grille lights are flashing.

"Medical Associates. May I help you?" Cassie May-baugh, Dr. Bloomgarden's wife and office manager, has answered the phone.

Mitchell can barely hear her: The Mozart is still playing, loudly. Pinching the phone between his jaw and collarbone, he turns off the radio and steers to the curb. In his mirror, he watches the police car pull over too. The cop puts on his hat, gets out of the cruiser, and slides his nightstick through the loop on the side of his wide belt.

"Hello?" Cassie says.

"Hi, uh, Cassie, this is Mitchell Taylor," he says, taking the phone in his hand again. "I'm afraid I'm running a few minutes late today." His chest tightens as he says the words.

"Hey, Mitch! Do you think you'll be in soon, or do you need to reschedule? Remember, Doctor B usually requires a twenty-four-hour notice for most cancellations."

Mitchell doesn't know what to say. He can't believe that Cassie would feel the need to remind him—Dr. B's best customer and, he's always felt, good friend—of their ridiculous cancellation policy while he's in the middle of a mini-crisis he has no control over. The policeman has walked over from his cruiser to Mitchell's car, and Mitchell holds up an index finger for him to wait.

"Sir, roll down your window, please," the cop says, his voice dull and muffled coming through the small gap at the top of the glass. A bull-necked giant, six and a half feet tall, he blocks the late-morning sun from shining into Mitchell's car, as if an overhead light has been flicked off.

"Yes," Mitchell says, and fumbles with the window's toggle switch. Because he's cut the engine, though, nothing happens.

"Yes, you're rescheduling?" Cassie says.

"Sir, put down the phone and open the window *now*." The cop has moved back a few feet and gripped his belt with both hands.

"Cassie, I'll call you back, I have to go," Mitchell says. He wants to explain further, wants to make it clear that he doesn't appreciate her patronizing treatment of him, but all he can think to say is, "Tell Doctor B I'll call back." He puts the phone on the passenger seat, unclips his seatbelt, and opens the door. "I have an appointment," he says to the cop.

"I need to see your license and registration, sir."

Mitchell wants the policeman to understand what's happening. He gets out of the car. "I need to be somewhere. That big SUV had me blocked in."

"Sit back down, sir, and let me see your license and registration," the cop says, stepping forward. "I'm going to have to cite you for using your cell phone while driving."

"But I didn't do anything wrong! I was just going to the doctor's. It was *those* guys." Mitchell points toward the underpass. "Didn't you see them?"

The cop keeps his eyes on Mitchell. "No, sir, I did not see them," he says, his chest now inches from Mitchell's face. "But it doesn't matter, because I saw *you*. Now, license and registration. Please."

⊹⊹⊹

Gwen meets Mitchell at the front door wearing her dusk-blue linen suit, one of the few business outfits she owns. Her hair is up in a loose bun. "How was your appointment?" she says.

Mitchell whips the citation out of his shirt pocket, ready to launch into his story, but notices the funny look on her face. "What's wrong?"

"Don't get upset, but there was, like, a *minor* incident with Henry and Craig Hightower at school." She glances down at her hands. "I just brought Henry home. He's in his room."

"You have *got* to be kidding me," Mitchell says, and hurries up the front stairs.

"He's okay," Gwen calls after him.

"He better be!"

At the end of the hall, Mitchell pushes Henry's door open. His son is sitting on the floor with an army of miniature toy soldiers set out in front of him.

Mitchell pushes his fists into his hips. "What happened at school?"

"Nothing, all right?" Henry says. He reaches into the clear plastic bucket beside him and scoops out another handful of men.

"No, not all right. What the hell happened?"

Henry jerks his head up; his father has never spoken to him this way before. "Nothing." His voice is very quiet, almost a whisper. "Craig kept hitting me at recess and then he was trying to tackle me and Jack. We said he wasn't allowed, but he did it anyway. Then I did what you said and told Ms.

Funk. But she said we were fighting, and then we had to go see Mr. Blackstone, and then Mommy had to come and get me."

Mitchell lets his breath go. He unclenches his fists and sits on the floor next to his son. "Okay, you did what I said, and I'm proud of you." He pauses, wanting to get his words just right. "But the next time that bully tries to tackle you or hurt you, tell him if he doesn't stop—and I mean right away—you're going to hurt *him*. And if he still doesn't stop, you punch him, okay? As hard as you can. Got it?"

Henry grins but then sees that his father isn't joking. His face drops and he nods slowly.

Mitchell has a short moment of regret, worried that he's scared his son, but he trusts that the feeling will pass. "So, what have you got here?" he says, eyeing the soldiers. "Can I play?"

Henry appears uncertain for a moment but then smiles. "Okay. Which ones do you want? There's blue and red men, and green army guys, and cowboys and Indians."

"Hmm, let's see." Mitchell begins organizing the figures, separating them into groups and subgroups, but stops himself and turns to Henry. "Actually, why don't you choose for both of us, Tigerman?"

As Henry forms two lines with the toys, Mitchell notices that the rows aren't exactly straight. He can tell without even counting that one side is going to end up longer than the other. But after watching his son for a minute—seeing his face tighten as he concentrates; noting how fluidly his small hands move from figure to figure; remembering how tiny those same hands and fingers looked in the incubator when he and Gwen almost lost their precious Henry— Mitchell leans back and keeps his mouth shut.

Reunion Update

FROM CASSIE MAYBAUGH'S "ME-TIME" BLOG

2016

First of all, a huge thanks to everyone who's worked their buns off to make the upcoming reunion possible. Thanks especially to **Archie Wagner** (Mr. Assistant Principal), who has been so helpful getting all the people and events coordinated and giving the reunion committee access to the school, where we're having the big dance on Saturday night. Love ya, Wags!

Remember, everybody, this is an All Alumni Affair, so whether you graduated from Brookford High in '78 (my year . . . 38! Can't believe it!) or last year—or any year before or in between—we hope you can make it. Go Bucks!

The theme for the picnic on Saturday afternoon is "Back in Brookford: Get Together for a Get-Together." We've heard from a lot of y'all that you're visiting town for the first time in years, so this is your chance to come on out and reconnect with old friends *and* make new friends and acquaintances. We're meeting at the top of Mount Warren from noon until 3:00, rain or shine. And BTW and FYI, we will not—I repeat, *not*—be stumbling around in the woods drunk and stoned out of our gourds this time. (Not that I ever knew anyone who would even think up such a thing!)

If you haven't been there lately, they've completed the renovations. Really, it is something, y'all. No more crumbling old picnic tables and overgrown trails. We're talking state-of-the-art facility, with a dance floor and dining area, and a glass-enclosed lookout tower, so you can see Brookford *and* Turnersburg *and* practically all the way over the mountains themselves. I'm really not kidding. And this is all without having to blaze a damn trail through the poison ivy and snake-infested forest. Also, the road has been paved and there's a nice big parking lot. So *please* bring your families. Kids, wives, husbands, significant others.

Oh, and one more thing. We've got updates on several folks who we hadn't heard from until the last few days. Some *can* make the reunion. Others, unfortunately, can't. But at least we have news, so here goes:

Christopher and Ruth Eastman can't make it (boo), but Ruth sends her best wishes and wants everyone to know that she's literally weeks away from opening her new catering business. She's calling it SIT DOWN AND EAT! Christopher, with his ever-expanding empire of craft-brew cafés and restaurants, will certainly be able to offer lots of sound business guidance—as if Ruth isn't as shrewd and savvy as they come. Anyway, more details on the way. (BTW, their son, **Daniel**, is doing *great*, according to Ruth. Rather than going into business like his father—and now his mother!—he's following in his grandfather's footsteps and will be teaching history at Cutler Prep this fall, which I think is super!) And even *more* exciting, Ruth has finally met *her* father, who sadly had been in prison for years. He tried to get in touch with Ruth after her mother died and she got placed in foster care, but he was never able to. Now, though, he's out and living in Montana, and somehow he and Ruth connected. So best wishes to Ruth and her long-lost dad.

Paul Storey, Brookford's favorite son, will be here for both the picnic *and* the dance. His new novel comes out in September. He says it's based on his experiences growing up in town, like many of his short stories and a few of his novels are. He also says he hopes everyone doesn't hate him after they read it. He admitted to me that he's glad the book isn't coming out *before* the reunion. Sooooo, we'll just have to wait and see what kind of Brookford dirt he dishes . . . all thinly veiled, of course. He does still want to write something about that guy who was stalking him all those years ago. (I really don't know what else to call it!) He told me that occasionally he's been tempted to simply publish all the emails the guy sent, but he doesn't know how that would go over. I tell you, living in New York City must be interesting, to say the absolute least. Anyway, say hi to Paul when you see him, but maybe don't say too much. You might end up in his *next* book!

Ian Drinkwater will also be here. He's still single (look out, single ladies) and coaching football at a high school outside Atlanta. He and Paul were always great friends growing up, and I know they'll be anxious to see each other. Ian's sister **Samantha**, of course, can't make it. She's still living with their parents and is still mostly unresponsive ever since she had that terrible stroke. Ian, though, says she seems to be comfortable and at peace, which is a blessing. I hope we will all continue to keep our beautiful friend in our thoughts and prayers. We love you, Sam!

I'm sorry to report too, in case you didn't know, that **Rose-Ann Jenkins** is starting another round of treatment. She's in good spirits, though, and vows to continue fighting this damn thing. **Jenks**, of course, is beside himself. He did call to say he'd really like to make the reunion, but he'll have to play it by ear, since he and Rose-Ann are having to take everything one day at a time. I'm sorry to be the bearer of this news, y'all. Please keep them in your prayers.

Wilson and Valerie Hopewell are back together and *will* make the reunion. A few years back, as you probably know, Wilson followed his dream of being a rock-band roadie and worked on the Marshall Tucker Band's reunion tour for a while. (So many reunions . . .) Well, "a while" turned into a good *long* while, which Val did not appreciate, especially with her boys, **Jeremy** and **Adam**, still at home (can't blame her). And anyway, oh my gosh, look at me airing everyone's dirty laundry. Shame on me! Anyway, they've made up, they are together, and their boys (*big* boys now) are doing great. So give them your best.

Bill and Patsy Patterson cannot come (again—boo), but we forgive them: They are still living in the big city and are traveling most of the summer to various wheelchair basketball tournaments, which have really been great for both of them. Billy—I mean Bill, sorry!—is apparently a star of the circuit these days, and Patsy enjoys the travel and the excitement of the games. Plus, I have no doubt that as Bill's manager, she loves the thrill of being in charge! We'll miss them, but I'm so happy that Bill and Patsy have something to be so passionate about in their lives. (Also, I need to say right here that I love, love, LOVE that Patsy took Bill's name. "Patsy Patterson" has got to be *the* most adorable name I think I've ever heard. I didn't take Dr. B's name—I am and will forever be Cassie Maybaugh, thank you very much—but if circumstances were different and I had the chance at a name even half as cute as Patsy's, I like to think I'd go for it!)

Before I forget, we also heard from **Curt Ralston**, who *can* make the reunion. He's had such a hard time of it, y'all, but he's doing okay these days. He's living near Spartanburg, SC, working at a rescue center for injured wildlife. And good news: According to Curt, his legal troubles are finally over. He is no longer a suspect in the fire that took his father, which was considered suspicious at the time. Glad they've left him alone now. So horrible that people would think he'd want to kill his own dad! Anyway, be sure to let Curt know you're happy for him at the get-together.

Gwen and Mitchell Taylor are going to try to at least make it to the dance. They're busy renovating their gorgeous place outside of town, turning it into an arts, yoga, and meditation center. Their son, **Henry**, who's a *very* talented carpenter and woodworker—as a lot of you know—is doing most of the work himself, which is *awesome* with a capital A.

And as *everyone* knows, Gwen is such an amazing artist. She's given up her greeting-card business and hopes this new space will attract "fine" artists from all over the area. Mitch has left his job too and plans to run the meditation and yoga side of the business. He expects to call it SHHHH, which is kinda unusual, but I think I like it! Let's all wish them well if we do see them.

BTW, I didn't know until recently that Gwen and Valerie Hopewell were, shall we say, a little wild in high school. (I guess we all were . . . a little.) Anyway, I didn't know them then—I'm old :(—but apparently they were real partners-in-crime back in the day, which I think is hilarious. Glad they survived (ha!), and so glad I've had the privilege of getting to know them now that we're all grown up.

Okay, kids, that's it. Dr. B and I can't wait to catch up with everyone. I hope we'll be able to do this again soon—maybe in another five years? If not, as soon as we can. If we have to wait ten years (or twenty or thirty) who knows where we'll all be, or if we'll even be around then! Sorry—morbid.

C U sooooon . . .

Honeysuckle

OLD MAN, SUMMER NIGHT

2045

Brookford, Friday night in June. Most folks home devicing the local news, local meaning Turnersburg, the larger gov-ship fifty kilometers up Route 063, where the data station makes its home. The late-night anchor is young, looks to be twenty-two going on sixteen. Strange how he reminds people in Brookford of Henry Taylor's teenage son—his oldest; his precious—killed this past March in a drunken fall off his grandparents' deckporch. For some, the resemblance is an odd comfort; others can hardly bear to look at their vuScreens. The anchor's narrow-boned face is too white in the glare of the studio lights, his custard-blond hair too stiff with truProd. So stiff it doesn't move in the least when he turns to make small talk with the weatherperson and, later, Our Very Own Dan-the-Man O'Callahan with Sports!

Out on Winchester Boulevard, teenage boys, and older buddies in their twenties who've never left the area, cruise across the county line in their jacked-up truTrux and buzzy cars. Out into the country darkness and then back into town, past the two digiMalls and Walmart World. Again and again and again. None of them understanding that this high-speed backing and forthing mimics what they'd like to be doing with the women who fill the glass pages of the vuDox slid under their mattresses. Knowing only that it feels good to guzzle nuBrew and stomp on the accelerator, whooping and hollering as the wind whips through their open windows.

Meanwhile, on the far side of town, in a truStone cottage at the end of a quiet lane—an elbow hook off Catalpa Place (itself a quiet, dead-end street)—the vuScreen has been on the fritz since 2037; the noises made by the teenage racers are nothing more than low rumbles. It's doubtful that the revving of the engines and the heavy sino-polk-funk pounding through backseat speakers—chest-rattling and dangerous-sounding up close, but white-noise benign at this distance—wake the old man. More likely, as usual, it's his wife—his second wife, nineteen years his junior—flat on her back beside him. For a moment, in his confusion as he arises from a dream, the old man wonders if her snoring is causing the bedroom's window curtains to move. She breathes out, and the truMesh drapes press against the screen. She breathes in, and they release and billow above the sill. But then he feels the breeze from outside.

The man is a light sleeper. His wife's snoring and sleep-talk whispering wake him practically every night. Not that he minds. He enjoys lying in bed, listening to the faraway traffic as though it were a river, staring up at the plasterized ceiling (eyes fully adjusted to the dark, no need to reach for the bedside lamp), and then getting up, shuffling in night-shirt and slippers across the braided rug and out of the room, easing the door shut behind him.

Through the kitchen, onto the slight tilt of the back deckporch, he retrieves the coffee can, box of matches, and half-pack of truSmokes he hides behind the glider sofa. The crack of a match head against the side of the sturdy box, and he lights his first sickoret. Pulls in the sweet smoke as he lowers himself onto the sofa and leans back. Certain his wife suspects his habit, but she's yet to catch him red-handed.

Eighty-two, been smoking on and off since he was thir-teen, not about to quit at this point in his life. Besides, he's down to four at these late-night sessions; what's the harm for an old man? Would be happy to tell anyone who'd lis-ten this very thing, even his wife. But he doesn't want to argue with her. Doesn't have the energy for it. Wouldn't be any fun.

He and his first wife, on the other hand—godness, the fun *they* had. The knock-down, drag-out battles, followed by the make-up sex on the kitchen table, him on his tiptoes, careful to avoid the blue and green shards of glass litter-ing the floor, all that remained of the bottles and jars she'd hurled. He knows this happened only once or twice but doesn't try to retool his memory. Prefers to believe that this kind of impulsive passion defined who and what they were.

No such passion with wife number two. Oh, she looks after him well enough—more than well enough: like a first-born golden child, making sure he's well fed, comfortable, content. And she's "peppy," a term his brother, Matt, liked to tease him with before he died driving home drunk from their wedding. But the old man worries: Beyond a simple appreciation for her companionship, there often isn't anything more.

Another drag off his sickoret, these thoughts swirling with the nicotine in his brain, unsettling him as usual. Blue smoke swirls above his head. Five miles away, under a half moon and a ceiling of stars, the red-eyed towers atop Mount Warren wink at him in slow motion. He rubs his bad leg and lets his breath go. Crushes the butt in the coffee can and lights another sickstick, cursing quietly. Why does he torture himself every night, talking himself out of love with wife number two, conjuring his dead first wife, his dead big brother?

All at once, though, the ghosts retreat as the wind gusts, carrying with it the scent of wild honeysuckle—the first he's noticed this year—from the overgrowth just beyond the stockade fence in his backyard. The aroma is relief. He sucks it in gratefully. In his eighty-two years, he's yet to hear a word more apt than "intoxicating" to describe honeysuckle's ability to soothe, to smooth over, with sudden, vivid remembrances: Summers more than sixty, seventy years ago. Grade school footraces through fields of long grass. Boyhood crushes; teenage lust—and rebellion. First love.

At that very moment, a quickening of his blood: whispers and laughter. He stubs out his sickstick and stills the motion of the glider. Watches with cat's eyes as a young couple emerges from behind the fence, holding hands, the old man struck by this coincidental vision, like a video from his youth. They make their way up the footpath that runs next to the cottage toward the lane, the boy sticklike, his voice echoing and teasing. The girl laughs and scolds in response. They stop to embrace before continuing along the path and out of sight. A minute later, doors slam in front of the cottage and car lights sweep the branches of the oak trees towering above the back deckporch.

The old man is briefly unsure if what he's just witnessed actually happened; almost sure he's not that senile. Is he still dreaming? He knows he isn't. He shakes his head and grins as he thinks about the couple. Then he fumbles with his half-pack of truSmokes, returns everything to its hiding place, and goes back inside.

By the time he's climbed into bed, the boy and the girl have reached the top of Catalpa Place, where they sit idling in the boy's brand-new beep-jeep. The boy lights a sickstick and peers through his windshield, blowing smoke, noticing the stars shining brilliantly. He puts the jeep in gear and steers toward the other side of town, the girl beside him, eyes on the road. After their special evening together—dinner at the Walmart nuCafe, followed by a romantic evening stroll, the early summer air soft and fragrant—she hesitates before whispering her secret.

The boy is silent at first; makes no sign whatsoever that he's heard her. Then flicks his sickoret out the window, showering orange sparks. He has plans, doesn't she understand that? He loves her but, godness, no way he's ready to be a father. His voice fills the small space as the beep-jeep flies faster and faster.

The girl begs him to slow down, just for one damn minute so they can talk, figure everything out. But he doesn't want to talk now, doesn't want to listen. He speeds along Kingley Avenue, Winchester Boulevard, and, minutes later, over the county line, turning to her again only when they've driven out into the country darkness. Grabs her wrist when she tries to interrupt and swerves into the path of the jacked-up truTrux and buzzy cars heading the other way, toward the digiMalls and Walmart World.

Emergency vehix on Winchester Boulevard. The data station's late-night anchor interrupts *The Tonight Show* with Breaking News from Brookford. But the old man—still called Jenks by those very few who've known him all his life—is unaware that any of this is happening: The sounds of traffic are no more than low rumbles along the lane where he lives; the vuScreen in the cottage has been on the fritz since 2037.

He lies awake, still picturing the young couple, grateful that their sudden appearance brought him to his senses, dissolving his obsessive thoughts of disappointment and death. He listens to his wife beside him, settled now, breathing quietly, and takes in the intoxicating scent of the wild honeysuckle, carried in on the breeze that causes the bedroom's window curtains to move.

ACKNOWLEDGMENTS

I would like to thank, with much love and appreciation, everyone who contributed their time and effort toward helping me create this "novel in stories" about a small Southern town.

I thank, especially, my wonderful family: my wife, Jenny Gillis, and our two children, Ellie and James Lott. The enthusiasm they've unfailingly shown for this project has meant the world to me. I love you all very much.

Thanks to my parents, Jim and Pam Lott. I have so appreciated my father's encouragement, as well as the writing advice and suggestions he's given me as he read, time and again, every piece I came up with. Sadly, my mother passed away in 2013, but she used to tell me how much she enjoyed even my more off-the-wall stories, and I will never forget that, or her. Love to you both.

Thanks too, for all their support, to my siblings and

their spouses—Mary Evans Lott, William and Sarah Lott, and Emily and Paul Miller—and their children. And to Jenny's family: my mother-in-law, Marcia Gillis, as well as my siblings-in-law and their spouses—Brendan and Jill Gillis, Gretchen Gillis and Dave Cook, Kathy Gillis and John Milcetic, Kevin Gillis, and Lorna Lyle—and all of their kids. Also to Becky and Joel Ginsburg, Bill and Catherine McCarty, Caitlin and Rob Mosesian, Boyd and Kim Purdy, Eric and Lauren Purdy, Jennifer and Jeff Miller, Andy and Shannon Vogt, Mary Pat Vogt, and their families.

Thank you, Anne Newgarden, Monique Peterson, and Kevin Sweeney, for your friendship, encouragement, and always insightful edits. Monique: I am so glad that you got us to start a writing group back in 2005. I owe a huge thanks too to the other members of our group—Sara Baysinger, Laura Cooper, Matthew Crain, Kathy Gillis, and Betsy Plowman—for the many, many reads and comments, and the fun we had. Anne and Kevin: Thanks for being there as the major "heavy lifters," reading draft after draft, revision after revision, of various stories and early versions of what would eventually become *Back in Brookford*. I offer my sincere thanks and appreciation also to Joshua Cohen, Laura Cooper, and Don Whitenack, all three of whom did more than their fair share of heavy lifting as well.

I will always be indebted to the following folks for reading my stories and giving me feedback: Diane Aronson, Ken and Laura Boward, Ellen Bryson, Anton and Sierra Byers, Anna Campbell, Rachel Deery, Ed and Andrea Ennis, Carrie and John Geer, Gretchen Gillis, Emily Gould,

Susan Groarke, Barbara Gulan, Gina and Matthew Hallock, Greg Hart, Michael Hensley, Karen Horton, Navorn Johnson, Barbara Jones, Jimmy and Mia Kivlighan, Ben Loehnen, Mary Evans Lott, William Lott, Lorna Lyle, Rachelle Mandik, Claire McKean, Bob Miller, Emily Miller, Jane Morriss, Caitlin Mosesian, Anne Cole Norman, Kelly Notaras, Patti Parsons, Kirk Obenschain, Walt Opie, Alex Rabb, Rob Riordan, Paul and Julie Sanger, Will Schwalbe, Jamie Sprunt, Renee Staab, Vincent Stanley, Dean Sullivan, Mary Pat Vogt, Emily Walters, Adam Weisblatt, Leslie Wells, Andrew and Charlotte White, and Anastasia and Jeff Zinkerman. Apologies to anyone I've missed. I send my thanks and best wishes to you too.

And thank you to Will Balliett, Elisabeth Dyssegaard, Amy Einhorn, Barbara Jones, Christine Kopprasch, Bob Miller, Kelly Notaras, Will Schwalbe, and Leslie Wells, for their wise counsel and practical advice.

To Michelle McMillian, for the striking text design and layout, and Dean Sullivan, for his artistic expertise creating the cover: Immense thanks to you both.

Thanks also to everyone at G&H Soho, especially Jim Harris and Gerry Burstein, for the care and attention to detail they put into producing the early "bound manuscript" version of the book.

To Drs. Richard Frank, Naveen Anand, Geoffrey Shapiro, and their respective staff members: Thank you for *everything*. You saved my life, and my family and I are forever grateful.

I want to acknowledge too those friends and family

members we've lost the last several years and who we re-member with great love and warm affection: John Gillis, Pam Lott, Sue Lott, Vernon Lott, Jim Lyle, Kirk Oben-schain, and Drew Vogt.

Last, here's to everybody who inspired me to create Brookford, a place I've come to love and where I've spent many happy times. Thank you all again.

ABOUT THE AUTHOR

DAVID LOTT is a writer and musician who grew up in Staunton, Virginia, in the heart of the Shenandoah Valley. These days, he lives in Connecticut with his wife, Jenny, and their two children, Ellie and James.

CPSIA information can be obtained
at www.ICGtesting.com
Printed in the USA
LVHW030427270722
724446LV00002B/278

9 780578 354880